BADASS HORROR

BADASS HORROR

Edited by Michael Stone and Christopher J. Hall

Dybbuk Press
http://www.dybbuk-press.org
New York, NY

Library of Congress Control Number: 2006921018

ISBN: 9780976654612

First Edition: June 2006

Cover Art and Illustrations by Federico Dallochio
Thanks to Vanessa Littlecrow Wojtanowicz

TABLE OF CONTENTS

POOL SHARKS
by Gerard Brennan

So, I'm in this bar in Wexford. Thing is, all the locals seem to
have a pool cue glued to their hands. I can't play pool very well.
In fact, when I pick up a cue it's because the fat end is going
into somebody's face. But this is my weekend break. I'm not
starting anything in here. I'm just gonna enjoy this here pint in
front of me. Maybe chase it with a little Jameson's Whiskey.
    My throat burns.
    It's funny how things never work out on holiday like you
expect them to. I have a cue in my hand and I'm staring down it.
The smooth wood rubs against the cleft of my chin as I try to
focus on the cue ball. Down here they call this a pressure shot.
The cue ball, the second last red and the pocket are all perfectly
in line. If I can just stop my bridging hand from shaking so
much it'll go down. I can smell the whiskey on my own breath
so I try to stop breathing. I'll be happy just to get to the black
ball before this bogtrotter clears the table and wins my fiver. At
least it will look like I put up a bit of a fight. Unsurprisingly, I
miss that gift of a shot and pot the white on the rebound.
Devastating. Not for the Wexford boy though. In fact he has a
great laugh as he sinks four yellows leaving the black lined up in
a shot that mirrored the one I just fluffed. He takes the black
then takes my fiver, smiling gleefully as he announces to the bar
that he has finally found someone who plays worse than he
does.
    I am not amused.
    "Double or nothing," I hear myself say.
    Wexford boy smiles as he looks to his friends at the bar. He
seems to be gauging the level of support available from the
crowd. I sense the greed as the calculation computes in the mind

of this Free State scumbag. He seems to like the odds.

"Sure thing, boy. Show me the money and rack them up."

I oblige eagerly. Surely it's about time that I win one game of pool. I mean, I always seem to beat myself and this guy had shown no real aptitude for the game. It's worth a shot. So I flash the cash and rack them up. I decide that I'm going to break, but Wexford boy is at the top of the table before I put down my pint glass. Cheeky fucker, wouldn't you say? I try to swallow and make vocal my protestations but the bastard has already connected with the cue ball. I see the small blue cloud of chalk dust and hear the knockout punch click as the white ball steams into the triangle. Two reds go down. This pisses me off. Red is my lucky colour. Plus I've been playing red in the last few games. It confuses me to change colours. I'll end up shooting at red and setting this bastard up for the win.

This seems like an inconsequential thought though. The fucker doesn't leave the table until there is only one red and the black remaining. I'd be hard pressed to think that I was any other colour but yellow. So I take my shot, a double whiskey without ice. Just to steady the nerves, like. Then I pick up the cue again. I try to formulate a sequence of shots that will reduce the gap a bit and leave the enemy snookered. Predictably enough the plan doesn't pan out. I miss the first ball I aim for and the white goes down.

There is a bit of a delay as the white gets stuck in the table for a while. The Wexford ingenuity prevails when the guy at the other table helpfully drops his white ball down the same pocket and both cue balls roll out. There follows a period of shock. Why didn't I think of that? I'll put it down to avoiding defeat.

They play two shot carry down here, so I've just given my foe two chances at a shot that could have been made by my five-year-old niece on a bad day. He decides to make me look worse by using just one shot to sink both the red and the black into opposite pockets. I suspect that this guy has a degree in advanced geometry. I'm not laughing and neither is the bogtrotter, but the rest of the establishment's clientele are sharing conspiratorial smiles. I begin to believe I've been had.

Wexford boy comes towards me with his hand extended. In a

show of good sport I go to shake it but the guy looks at me like I have fifty-two heads. Then I realise that he wasn't trying to be my pal. He wanted to be paid. I take the note from my pocket and utter a prayer of thanks that the lack of lighting in this place hides my blushing cheeks. The darkness doesn't do anything for the feeling of defeat though. It doesn't help my paranoia either. I imagine the locals sniggering into their beers and making obscene gestures behind my back. Just another smart arse northerner taken on by a bunch of hillbillies he felt superior to half way through the first pint. Pretty fucking embarrassing, if I do say so myself.

"Give us another go, mate." I am astounded to hear these words coming from my own mouth. This has to be pride talking. Maybe insanity.

"I will in me stones," says he. (That means no, right?)

If I were in a better mood just then I would have laughed at that eloquent phrase. Instead I feel fury rising in my gut like lava. This ugly gap-toothed southerner had made me look like an idiot and now he didn't even have the decency to show me some manners. Not even a chance to win back the money I lost. I feel my grip tighten around the pool cue. I survey my surroundings in anticipation of the murderous swing I'm about to deploy in the general direction of this fuck's head. It looks like there is plenty of room. This boy's head is split.

But then he surprises me.

"Come on ye fucker ye," he announces. "I'll buy ye a drink."

He turns his back to me and moves towards the bar leaving me speechless. When he senses that I'm not following, he looks over his shoulder.

"Ye can leave that stick behind and all," He says, "Give some other northerner a chance to lose some money."

I almost crack a smile.

As I walk towards the bar my face cools and I feel my tensed body relax. Maybe this guy isn't too bad after all. I might even like him a little. It *is* pretty impressive how he acts like a right 'Paddy know nothing' until he gets on the table. Then this clumsy slope shouldered youth we see before us turns into sharp and sleek cat among the pigeons. Kind of remarkable, really.

Might be good to get to know someone like him. Useful for future projects and the like.

I get to the bar and my new friend hands me a double whiskey sans ice. I'm impressed by his observational skills. Real nice guys always know what you're drinking. So we get to talking and it turns out that Wexford boy's name is actually Ronan. Nice to meet you Ronan, and all the rest. The usual shit is talked about football, cars, women and the political state of Northern Ireland. Basic conversational topics throughout the whole island, three of which are universal topics throughout the world. Well, Europe anyway. I'm guessing that Attila the Hun wasn't a Manchester United fan.

Before I realise it, Ronan has bought me another whiskey. That's the first fiver he won gone already. I have a bit of a problem understanding this method of moneymaking, but to be honest I really don't give a fuck as long as the whiskey keeps flowing. I finish the second drink as Ronan polishes off the last of his first. The second pool table is empty again and both of us are eyeing it up.

"Fancy a quick friendly?" asks Ronan.

I nod my agreement and we head to the table. Ronan offers me the break and I take it. Crunch! I make an impressive scattering and amaze myself when two reds go down. I imagine the rest of the bar raising a collective eyebrow but this is merely fantasy. They are all much too concerned with their own drinks and conversations. Fools, they will fail to witness my first sporting achievement south of the border. Well it's their loss, its time for me to shine.

I stay on the table and sink seven reds off the break. The black hangs over the lip of the pocket bottom right of the table. I could win this. I take my time stalking round the table examining every possible angle. Ronan leans on his cue, a bemused smile creasing his face. As he lights a cigarette I finally decide on the direct approach. The cue ball rolls slowly towards the black. Fear rises as I realise that the shot isn't going to connect.

But it does. Ever so gently the two balls kiss and the black gracefully totters over the edge. The sound of that elusive orb rolling about inside the table is music to my ears. I calmly set the cue down on the table then do an enthusiastic Irish jig while singing "Ole, ole, ole, ole, oh lay oh, oh lay!" This may be the proudest moment of my life.

Ronan looks quite amused by the whole spectacle. I begin to realise that a lot of people have started watching me and I slowly come to a stop, my last dance step punctuated by an inaudible "ole?" Still the embarrassment doesn't last long as I am challenged by someone from the bar. Then another and another. I win, I win, and I win. This is unbelievable. I'm like a man possessed. I'm afraid to take a drink in case it quells the buzz. Holy shit, I am on fire!

It isn't long before people start queuing up to play for money. At first I am tentative about this. I fear that my winning streak will end if money depends on the outcome, but I want to stay on the table. They won't let me stay on unless I start playing for money. I win though and I continue to win until the barman shouts for last orders. The locals persuade the barman to keep on serving in the ancient tradition of the "Irish lock in." By this stage, I am already holding a fair bundle of notes and I'm still on top of my game. The challenges keep coming and I continue to accept each victory with grace. (The dancing was becoming quite unpopular by the fourth game. Bit of a surprise really.) Before long I look at my watch. It's two thirty in the morning and I haven't had a drink since eleven. My mouth is starting to get dry and I'm getting pissed off. I feel like I am chained to this table and doomed to serve for eternity, entertaining these bumpkin fucks. I need a drink, now!

I consider throwing a game but pride prevents me from doing so. I take a quick look around to see if there is anyone left to play and realise that I have played every customer here. Even the barman has tried and failed before being called to top up the pints. They kept on trying though and only about three challengers have managed to get a shot. By two forty-five I announce that enough is enough and I need a drink. They seem a bit disappointed, so I cheer them up by handing the barman one hundred euros from my winnings and request that drink be served to all on the premises until the money runs out. They look at me like I'm a saint, not really getting the fact that I'm using their money. But then maybe I'm being soft. To quench my own thirst I buy a full bottle of Jameson's from the optical and retreat to a table in the corner with a glass and get stuck in. I feel the comforting burn in my throat as the magic attacks my stomach. My God this is great. It could be one of the best weekends ever.

I have taken a good chunk from my private bottle and I'm starting to get a little bit drunk. I can feel the heat of the whiskey lighting up my face. The power of it courses through my veins and it feels good, but as I stand up to make my way to the toilet, I sway a little. Nobody notices though. In fact, I realise that there are only four people left in the bar. I thought this was a lock in. How did they all get out? On my way to the toilet I notice a fire exit at the back of the bar. That explains the amazing disappearing dickheads. I continue on my merry way.

The whiskey paranoia takes me into a cubicle to relieve myself. One thing I hate about urinals is the vulnerable position they leave you in. Anybody can attack you from behind and the one thing worse than getting a hiding is pissing all over yourself while you get a hiding. I've seen it happen and it isn't a pretty sight.

The cubicle I choose doesn't have a lock on the door so I adopt some drunken gymnastics. Standing on one leg with the other pressed firmly against the door I let it flow. Admittedly, most of it hits the cistern and soaks the floor, but at least I don't hit my shoes. I zip up, rinse my hands on the way out and retreat to my bottle.

Unfortunately, the mood in the bar seems to have changed quite a bit. Ronan is shouting at some guy. There seems to be a large fresh beer stain on the back of Ronan's blue shirt. His face has gone red and now he is jabbing at the other guy's chest with his index finger. This is usually not a good thing, so I move to the pool table and lift a pool cue.

Another fellow spots me doing this but gets the wrong idea. He tries to get me to play him. I recognise him from earlier as Ronan's cousin who can't play for shit but isn't a bad chap. I politely refuse and point out that Ronan may be in a spot of trouble. Mickey, I think his name is, looks over at the heated discussion-turned-pushing match. He doesn't look too bothered though. He continues to insist that we have a rematch.

Now, I don't know if this applies to many people, but when I drink a little too much whiskey I sometimes go to a dark place. This transition usually occurs just after three quarters of a bottle. As far as I remember, I haven't had much more than half a bottle but I can feel the dark place creeping up on me. It seems to come from behind my eyes and steal my memories. It makes me into half the man I want to be. The bad half. The violent half. The remorseless half.

I walk towards the scuffle with purpose. Things go black.

Wet and freezing, things come back into focus. I'm not sure where I am or what the fuck is going on now. I realise that I can't move my arms. I can't move my legs either. This is not a good thing. I figure out that I have just been woken by a pint glass of ice-cold water in the face. I blink as much of the offending liquid out of my eyes as I can before looking around for a friendly face. I can tell that I'm lying on top of one of the pool tables because the high wattage light fixture that hangs above them is burning my eyes out. I hear a familiar voice.

"Bit violent, aren't ye?"

It's Ronan's voice, but it has a crisp quality to it. He does not seem to be amused. His face is now in my vision, haloed by the pool table lights. He seems to be bleeding. I can still move my head and I can see the other guys in the bar. Mickey is still there and the big guy that was giving Ronan a hard time is too. They are the only ones I can see but I can hear the rattle and clink of glasses from the bar and figure that the barman is still on the premises too. What I still can't figure out, though, is why I can't seem to move any of my limbs or sit up.

"What's happening here?" I ask in the toughest voice I can muster. It isn't that tough.

"Ye went a bit off the rocker, pal." Says the big man, "We had to put you down for the night. It's your own fault, ye know. No need for that sort of behaviour at all."

I'm still at a loss. The last thing I remember is going to the aid of my new friend Ronan. Now my good friend and the man

I tried to save him from look like a couple of good friends looking at one of the less exciting animals in the zoo. I need a bit more information here. I ask for it.

"Well you see," starts Ronan, "ye tried to take the head off me Brother Jimmy here with one of our own pool cues. That just isn't on, ye know? So we made sure ye couldn't hurt anyone else for the night. Me Cousin Mickey had a length of rope out in his car there so we tied you to that pool table you're so fond of. Time for a bit of schooling now, boy."

With that, Ronan, Jimmy and Mickey move out of my field of vision, and again my eyes scream in pain as the unforgiving light assaults them. I want to close them, but the noises I hear keep them open as I try to stay alert and guess what is coming next. The only thing that I can be sure of is that it will not be good. I can hear what sounds like a cane being whipped around in the air. It is not one of your more pleasant sounds when you are tied to a pool table in a small pub in a rural part of Wexford knowing that nobody who gives a shit about you knows where you are. The other sound is laughter. Not the raucous kind of laughter that is usually associated with bars, but more the laughter of cruel adolescents torturing defenseless animals with fireworks. I start to shake with fear and only willpower of the highest degree holds my bladder in check.

My eyes get a temporary reprieve as Ronan's face once again enters my field of vision. It seems to have gotten uglier and it now wears a sneer. He starts to yell, and as he does spittle flies from his mouth and most of it lands on my face. It takes me a while to decipher the message but I start to realise that he is saying the same thing over and over.

"We'll teach ye, you're just a little fucker. We'll soon teach ye, you're just a little FUCKER!"

It goes on and on like a medicine man's chant. Just as I begin to realise things are going to get worse very soon the real pain starts. The whisper of something cutting through the air and a searing pain across my beer gut informs me that I am bare-chested. As I scream in shock and agony Ronan's chant goes up in volume like some evil and discordant melody reaching its crescendo. As my scream starts to boil down to a breathless whimper, the sound whickers through the air again and hits the same spot. The agony explodes and seems to be double that of the original. Trying with all my might to grit my teeth against the scream I focus my attention on the source of my torture. I see that Jimmy is administering the treatment and that his weapon of choice isn't a bamboo cane but the top of a fishing rod. He sees me looking at him and traces a circle in the air with the rod before lashing down on my gut again. His aim is devastatingly accurate as he plants it in the same spot for a third time. The man was obviously born for this.

I know I need to focus if I want to get away from the pain but it seems useless. There isn't a thing I can do about it. I'm no Harry Houdini or even a David Blaine. I'm just a smartarse northerner at the mercy of some psychotic bumpkins. Mickey places himself opposite Jimmy and now he seems to be holding the other half of the fishing rod. He smiles at me and I foolishly think that he might just save me. I realise just how much I misread this guy as he nods to Jimmy and the blows rain down on my stomach in alternating strikes. It takes me a second to realise that I'm screaming at the top of my lungs. This realisation does little to help my situation and I start to black out.

Just as the merciful depths of unconsciousness begin to claim me, my face is soaked again. This time Ronan doesn't bother taking the ice out of the glass. He continues to scream his bizarre mantra, but his voice is beginning to crack. Jimmy and Mickey also seem to be feeling the effects of their physical exertion. The whipping begins to slow down to a stop.

"Had enough?" I ask, but they don't seem to hear me. I've lost a little volume after all the screaming.

Ronan stops screaming and asks the other two if they fancy a drink. After nodding their affirmation they move towards the bar and out of my field of vision. I can feel the stickiness of drying blood on my stomach but it seems to be numbing against the pain. I can hear the sound of liquid being poured and try to reassess my situation. I hear footsteps approaching me and Ronan is beside me again. He is holding a jar of pickled onions.

"Don't worry, pal, we haven't forgotten ye."

He twists the lid off the jar and pours the contents onto my lacerated skin. The pain reaches a new level. I can't even scream. Instead of blacking out there is an explosion of light to accompany the agony. I begin to convulse and pull at the ropes that bind me to the table. I start to think that this pain will never end, but the numbness starts to creep in again. As this happens I start to become aware of the maniacal laughter from the torturous trio. I wonder where the bartender has gone as I can't pick out the sound of his movements and his voice hasn't mingled with the others. I begin to construct a fantasy of salvation at the hands of a landlord who has been pushed too far. It doesn't get time to develop. My three captors are in my face again, looking even more sadistic and cruel than before.

"Have ye learned your lesson yet, pal?" Ronan asks.

I try to croak a response and they seem to consider my case amongst themselves. There is a lot of shrugging and head shaking going on but as long as they aren't hitting me this is a good thing. Then it seems to be Jimmy's turn to speak.

"We have a proposition for you, pal. We'll untie you now if you agree to behave yourself. Do ye think ye can do that? Well I think ye can, but Mickey here doesn't trust ye. Now don't disappoint me, pal. I really hate to lose a bet."

With that the three of them begin to loosen the ropes. Ronan and Mickey take an arm each and Jimmy attends to the rope around my legs. I briefly entertain the idea of planting a kick right onto the bridge of Jimmy's nose, but it seems to die out as quickly as it occurred to me. The ropes are gone and Ronan and Mickey help me to a sitting position. They guide me towards the edge of the table, and as my feet touch the floor they let go of me. I immediately crash to the floor.

"Told ye he had no fight left in him," says Jimmy.

"Better pay the man, Mick," Ronan adds.

With a bit of muttering Mickey moves towards Jimmy and hands him a few notes. I'm too wired on pain to be able to take in how much the bet is worth. It doesn't seem important anyway. I try to get to my feet, and make it on my third attempt by using the pool table for support. The three just watch. Once again money changes hands. This time it goes to Ronan. Now that I'm on my feet I look at the damage they have inflicted. I can hardly believe that this is my body. My stomach is a mess of angry bleeding welts and I notice that the skin around my wrists is raw and bleeding too. The pain around my ankles informs me that things aren't much better there.

The boys look at me expectantly. I still don't trust myself to speak, so I attempt a shrug. The pain that accompanies the movement makes me promise myself not to do it again. I have no way of knowing how long I was tied to the table but I suspect that we are now well into the morning after the night before. Still the boys watch me and I watch back. Finally Ronan speaks.

"It's time for another game of pool."

I continue to look at them. I have no idea what to say. I need to make sure that I can still speak though.

"Can I sit down?" Spineless, but a start nonetheless.

"Ye can in your stones" Ronan says, "If you sit down ye won't get up again. Look at the state of ye. I said it was time to play pool didn't I? Ye can't play on your arse, or are ye better than ye let on?"

"I don't understand," I begin.

"Shut the fuck up!" Jimmy yells. "I'm going to rack them up and you're going to play against Mickey. Ye don't get a choice, but ye do get a chance. If ye win we let ye go. If ye lose we kill ye. Don't try to understand, just get ready to play."

"But why?" I ask.

"What did I tell ye?" Jimmy screams and moves towards me.

I seem to be stuck to the floor, waiting for him to hit me. Instead he grabs my left wrist in one hand and my index finger in the other. There is a dry snapping sound as my index finger is bent back and broken. I can't take it anymore and throw up on the floor. I notice that there are traces of blood in the vomit and start to heave again. My tormentors begin to cheer me on.

"Guess we should use the other table then boys," suggests Mickey. "This one's fucked."

The others agree and the sound of the pool balls being racked up is the only sound for a while. I begin to sway on the spot, but before I am given the luxury of falling down I am manhandled in the direction of the other table. As I am turned around I catch a glimpse of my face in the mirror behind the bar. It looks as if my stomach wasn't the only thing that was worked over. My face looks like it was bounced against the floor for a few hours before I gained consciousness. It probably was.

I am left at the end of the table and Ronan puts a cue in my hand. I really look at the three amigos for the first time since I realised I was tied to the pool table, and I notice that they too look like they've been in the wars. Ronan is limping as he moves towards a bar stool and one of Mickey's cheekbones seem to have dropped a little, making him look a bit like a stroke victim. Jimmy's shirt collar looks to be drenched in his own blood and, as he turns to the bar to pick up a bottle of beer, I can see a nasty gash running down the middle of the back of his head. It runs in a perfectly straight line and to me looks like the kind of injury you get from a well-placed pool cue. I almost feel proud.

"If ye use that pool cue for anything but its intended purpose during this game, pal, yer dead." This information is relayed by the ever diplomatic Jimmy. I nod my agreement, but I'm beginning to feel a little bit more like myself now.

I look to Mickey and he signals for me to break. I am suddenly and painfully reminded that I have a broken finger as I rest the cue on my thumb and forefinger. I scream, much to the delight of Ronan, Jimmy and Mickey. I find I am coming to terms with my pain now, though. I try to gain control again and think. I also improvise a new way of cradling my cue. It makes my hand look like a crippled animal. It's the best I can do though, so I line up the break. I connect well with the cue ball but the angle is bad. The triangle barely separates.

"Ah, bad luck, pal," Mickey says as he chalks up his cue. He bends over the table to take his shot and the pack separates. Nothing gets sunk though. The others laugh as I sway on my feet trying to concentrate on the green felt. I feel a shove from behind as I am prompted to take my shot. I should be able to hit something. There seems to be thirty balls on the table. Now if they would just stop moving I should be able to take an early lead.

I line up another shot and the pain shooting up from my

hand makes me scream again. The three psychos scream even louder in mock chorus. The taunts only make me more determined however, and I almost smile as a red ball makes its way to the pocket. It topples lazily over the lip and runs the lap of victory around the inside of the table. They fall silent for a few seconds in disbelief. I turn to look at them and realise for the first time that Ronan is videotaping the game.

He turns the camera on Mickey and begins to laugh. Jimmy starts laughing too, but Mickey looks less than amused. He steps toward me with intent but is held back by the others.

"Don't be like that Mickey. Give the man a chance to finish the game. That's the deal, remember?" says Ronan.

Mickey's expression softens a little as he lets this sink in. Then he smiles and begins to nod. He doesn't speak but points to the table, indicating that I should take my next shot. I look to Ronan and I'm confronted by the lens of the camera. Jimmy stands next to him rubbing his hands together and sniggering. With nothing to lose now I decide to chance my luck.

"Do you think I could have a whiskey to help me concentrate?" I ask.

"Jesus but this man is desperate, would you boys be thinking about drink at a time like this?" asks Ronan. He points his camera first to Jimmy who looks back at it with a theatrical expression of shock and then to Mickey who is nodding his head slowly with a hangdog expression. None of this is getting me any closer to the whiskey though. I tap the butt of my cue on the floor in a bid for attention. As they look at me I raise a cupped empty hand to my lips and raise my eyebrows. This takes a considerable amount of effort, but I believe that it's worth it. I need that whiskey to make me stronger and get me through the pain.

"Looks like he's getting impatient there, Ronan," says Jimmy.

The three of them look at me with something close to fondness. Ronan goes to the bar and reaches for a bottle of Black Bush and a clean glass. It's not my brand but I don't have the energy to argue. I remember how I was impressed at the start of the night by Ronan getting my drink right without any prompting, and believe that this is just another psychological blow. He puts the glass down near the pool table and leaves the bottle standing beside it. He removes the bottle cap but doesn't pour it. I stumble towards the whiskey in gut-wrenching agony, biting my tongue to stop me screaming. I use my right hand to lift the bottle and pour. Some hits the table, but I manage to half fill the glass and put the bottle back on the table without too much pain. I grab the glass and drain it. Thank God!

I turn back to the table and with a renewed determination see my next three shots. I dream of a perfect game and a happy ending. To think of anything else is too dangerous. I take my shot, careful not to rest the cue on my broken finger. I sink it. I move immediately to my next shot and sink one again. I line up another one. I hold my breath as the cue ball makes its way to the target and moan in despair as the fourth red ball moves an inch then stops before the lip of the pocket. All my hopes crumble and I begin to notice the pain again. I move towards my whiskey and realise that the Three Amigos are no longer taunting me. They are looking at me in astonishment.

"I wasn't expecting ye to put up such a fight," Ronan says. "I'm impressed."

I'm less than flattered and continue towards my whiskey. My knees buckle as I reach for the bottle and knock it over. It rolls off the table and shatters. It's the final straw and I begin to sob. I turn to the Wexford boys, ready to abandon all pride and beg for another bottle. Mickey and Jimmy look disgusted by my performance but Ronan seems to understand my plight.

"Go ahead fellah. Help yourself." He points towards the bar.

I wipe the tears from my eyes and try to straighten up as best I can. I know that there is no way I can reach across the bar for my bottle without stretching my wounds so I go behind it. I look for Jameson's first then laugh to myself for being so fussy. I reach for a bottle of Jack Daniel's instead. As I turn to go back to the game I notice something so interesting I nearly forget about my injuries. The barman obviously has a few security concerns because he has a double barrel shotgun under the bar. I look towards the till for a panic button or silent alarm, but quickly realise that the gun is my only chance. For some reason this makes me even happier. I lean on the bar, looking down at the gun as I try to gather my strength.

"Come on, dickhead!" Jimmy shouts. "Let's finish this game."

I look at them and see that Mickey is looking at the pool table thinking about his next shot, while Jimmy looks at me impatiently and Ronan points the camera in my direction. I decide I need to act now. I reach for the shotgun and point it at the space between Jimmy and Ronan. Ronan lowers the camera and looks at me in disbelief. Mickey drops his cue and puts his hands in the air. I rest the barrel on my forearm to avoid jarring my broken finger.

"You can let me go or I can kill you," I announce in the strongest voice I can muster.

Although Jimmy is obviously as shocked as the others, I'm not surprised that he is the first one to speak.

"Ye stupid fucker ye. There's two cartridges in a double-barrel shotgun and there's three of us. Do ye understand what that …?"

His sentence is cut short by a shotgun blast. Jimmy's head explodes and his remains slump to the floor. I swing the barrel towards Ronan who is now the closest man to me. He hardly notices as he is looking at his brother's body. Mickey only has eyes for me. I'm pretty sure he is going to stay put so I speak again, mostly for Ronan's benefit.

"You can let me go or I can kill you. Who's next?"

Ronan snaps out of his trance and give me a look of pure hatred. He begins to move towards me, and although I should just shoot him, I try to reason with him.

"Ronan, I will kill you if you take one more step in this direction."

"Mickey, ye make sure ye kill this cunt when he shoots me. Do ye hear that?"

As he says this, he closes his eyes and starts walking towards me. I look towards Mickey and see that he is also advancing with his pool cue in his hands. I need to act. The gun goes off in my hand again. Ronan screams but Mickey doesn't make a sound. Instead he looks down at his tattered chest and drops his cue again. Ronan looks down at his own body first then turns in time to see Mickey collapse. As he turns back to me again I hurl the bottle of Jack Daniels at him. It hits him in the face and I almost retch at the sound of his nose breaking. He goes down screaming.

I begin to move while I still have time and strength. As I make my way to the fire exit I noticed earlier I use the shotgun for support. I try to speed up as a crashing sound behind me indicates that Ronan is trying to get to his feet. Just as I think I'm about to make it the shadows come to life and the barman emerges with a baseball bat resting on his shoulder.

"Where the fuck were ye?" Ronan screams from behind and he sounds close. I whimper at the sheer volume. "Ye let this cunt kill my brother and my cousin and ye didn't do a thing. What the fuck?"

The barman says nothing to defend his actions but walks towards me. I try to look him in the eyes to plead with him, but he seems to be looking through me. I get ready to get knocked out again and know that this time I will not be waking up. I grit my teeth but the barman walks past me. I hear a dull thud as the bat connects with Ronan's head and a crash as he hits the deck. I turn to look at my saviour and he looks back at me. He doesn't look angry, just defeated.

"You earned your freedom, son," he says. "I can't let these boys rule my life anymore. I can't sleep anymore because all I hear is screaming. You were far from the first fellah to get caught up in this shit, but you'll be the last. I need to earn my

soul back. You need to get out of here and thank Jesus for the strength he gave you. I've never seen one of their victims actually try to play the game. They just break down. But you're the last. You get to keep your life. You win, son. Go home and thank Jesus because I could swear I'd left that gun unloaded. My father always taught me to be careful."

I continue to look on however and the barman swings the bat downward, connecting with Ronan's skull. There is a sickening crack. I overcome my desire to throw up and breach the shotgun. There are no spent cartridges in the barrels.

I walk towards Ronan's body as the barman prepares to swing again. The barman stops and looks at me warily, but I don't have enough strength to tell him about the gun. Instead, I just point to the camera, which is still in Ronan's hand. The barman understands what I want but seems to take a second to think about it. He makes his decision and hands me the camera, and in return I hand him back the gun that saved my life. He rests the gun against the table, gives me a tortured smile and turns back to Ronan.

Once again I move towards the fire exit stepping in time with the thudding blows raining down on Ronan's body. I need that camera you see. No one is going to believe my story without it. I need to be believed, especially if I intend to help the barman earn back his soul.

I swing open the fire exit door and I'm bathed in morning light. I wish I'd lifted the bottle of whiskey as well though.

THE STRAY
by Garry Kilworth

No one remembers why Lavinia allowed Tom to remain in the cat house, not even Kitty. He certainly didn't do any work, not even a little sweeping up. Tom was simply *around*, sitting by the bar, curled up in a chair by the big open fire, or wandering the house quietly with that soft smile on his face, saying "Hi," to everyone he met. Even the customers didn't seem to mind a tame male wandering in accidentally while they were desperately trying to get their money's worth.

"It's only Tom," the girl would say, taking the opportunity of the respite to adjust some flimsy piece of underwear. "Off you go, Tom, we're busy." And the man would grunt and go back to work, leaving Tom to wander out again.

No one actually knew where Tom had come from in the first place. He just turned up on the doorstep and Kitty, whose job it was to bring in the morning papers, found him there. Kitty was one of those people who love all pathetic creatures, couldn't bear to see a living thing in sorrow or pain, and just had to cherish the unwanted. She took him a glass of warm milk, persuaded Lavinia to allow Tom to stay to breakfast, and after that he seemed to become a fixture.

Kitty herself was small and delicate, with pale, translucent skin: a gossamer fairy with tiny features. All the big, shambling men with clumsy limbs wanted Kitty. Lavinia would tell them, "You stay underneath, you hear? I don't want you crushing our little Kitty," and they would nod their great dome heads slowly and solemnly in dumb assent, or make some sound like a truck changing gear, which meant yes.

It was Kitty's duty to see that Tom was fed, and she insisted he take a shower once a week at least. When he first arrived he was covered in fleas, but Kitty got some stuff from the drugstore and deloused him. Apart from that, he was left pretty much alone, to drape himself over a piece of furniture in whatever part of the great old clapboard house he happened to be at the time. He was just *there*.

Kitty did ask Tom once where he was born and raised and he mumbled something about, "The wrong side of the tracks," and that was the closest they ever got to his origins.

Life in the whore house suited Tom's habits and peculiarities. Tom was a night person, often sleeping until early evening, mostly on the pool table, his favourite bed. Occasionally he would accompany one of the girls down to the supermarket. He wouldn't *do* anything, like carrying shopping: if ever he was asked he looked panic stricken and helpless. Once, when Sasha tried to put some groceries in his arms, he dropped them all over the sidewalk. Sasha shouted at him when they got back to the house and Tom disappeared for a while. Kitty found him sleeping on the logs in the lean-to woodshed, the next day, and only her soothing voice managed to get him to enter the house proper again. For a while after that, whenever Sasha came into the room, Tom would slink out quickly.

One of the few times Tom was really useful was when there was a problem in the kitchen. Baby Jane and Rita were washing the dishes after lunch one day when Baby Jane screamed and pointed at the trash bin. An unmistakable ugly tail was visible, the body of its owner hidden by the bin.

"A rat!" she shrieked.

Rita dropped the dish she was wiping it smashed to pieces on the floor. Both women ran from the kitchen screaming. The noise brought Lavinia, the rest of the girls, and Tom.

When the girls told Lavinia what was the matter, Tom, without a word, went to the bar. He reached under the counter and took out the axe handle which Bud used to subdue drunks and violent customers. Then he padded straight into the kitchen, while Lavinia and the girls stared after him. There were the sounds of scuffles, a solid thump, and then Tom came out grinning, dangling the rat by the tail.

Kitty laughed, and said, "Tom's got a present for you,

Lavinia," and the madam laughed too.

Occasionally, Tom would go out at night. No one knew where he went, but Kitty said he just walked the streets. "He gets restless, cooped up in here all the time," she said. "It's natural to want to get some air once in a while — no harm in that."

The law brought Tom home one night, telling Kitty they'd found him out in the back yard of a married woman's house, watching her getting undressed through the window. They were brought before the six-foot tall Lavinia, who had the nose and eyes of an Egyptian Queen, and were naturally uneasy beneath her imperious gaze. They felt like boys snitching on a classmate.

"The woman looked out of her window and there he was, down below, skulking amongst the trash cans," said the first officer.

"The guy's a peeping tom," said the second officer.

Lavinia thought that was funny, especially considering Tom's name and all. "Hey," she said, "he's surrounded by girls taking their clothes off — why would he want to watch some thick-waisted housewife baring her ass, when he's got all these lovely ladies doing just that the whole while?"

The officers, looking around them greedily at the girls packaged in purple negligees, satin panties and bras, and exotic wraps, agreed that it was something of a puzzle.

"Well, what the hell *was* he doing then?" the second officer asked.

Kitty answered this question. "He was probably going through the trash cans," she said. "He likes to do that. He finds things and cleans them up — uses them as gifts for us girls."

"Well," said the first officer, "we'll overlook it this time, but you watch it, Tom, you hear?"

And Tom obediently nodded his head and smiled.

The officers both had freebies and everyone was happy except the housewife. Lavinia, who knew much about most inhabitants of the town, was aware of illicit meetings between the housewife and a guy who delivered fish on Thursdays. One telephone call was enough to get the woman to drop the complaint about Tom.

Then there was the time Tom got lost, down amongst the railway workers' shacks on the east side of town. The girls went out in pairs looking for him, with Lavinia becoming more impatient by the day, saying, "If he's not found soon, you'll have to forget him — and Kitty, for heaven's sakes stop sniffling — the customers are tired of seeing your nose running." They discovered him in some man-starved widow's house and demanded his return. The widow eventually let him go saying he didn't 'do anything' anyway, except for eating and sleeping, and in her opinion wasn't a great deal of use to a body.

Tom, tousle-haired and fatter on fried food, followed the girls obediently back to the whore house.

Kitty gave Tom a strong talking to while he shuffled and hung his head and promised *never* to do it again.

Despite the incident with the rat in the kitchen, Tom was not inclined towards violence, in fact he ran from it. If there was a fight between drunks, or a heavy argument over a payment, Tom would creep away somewhere to hide. Even when Kitty was involved in something, and could have used his protection, Tom was not forthcoming. Kitty said it wasn't because Tom was a coward, or afraid, he just did not see why he should get involved in a battle which did not directly concern him. If someone picked on him, or harassed him in any way, why that was a different matter. A grinning sailor tried to get Tom to give him a piggyback one night, blocking the doorway when Tom wanted to leave the room, and Tom eventually tore into the man. The sailor needed three stitches to sew a fingernail wound on his cheek.

Tom, then, was a warm, comfortable person to have around in a place where there was a lot of unhappiness. One or two of the girls had chosen the life they led, but the majority of them had been forced into it by poverty and necessity, or by unscrupulous men who fed on women. Sasha, dark-haired, dark-eyed, had a heroin habit and she found the easiest way to get the money to satisfy it was on a bed. Patty, a black girl from out of town, had been beaten by her lover into street walking, and had taken refuge in a lesser evil by running away and going into an established house. Kitty had just been plain poor, a girl born in a mountain shack, raped by her brother when she was 11, devoid of education. Others had similar reasons for going into the oldest profession.

Tom was someone, a *man*, these girls could all talk to and he would listen sympathetically and nod his head.

"Bad," he would say quietly. "Bad."

They told him all their woes; vilified ex-lovers and ex-husbands; were damning of all governments, systems of justice, law officers, pimps and pushers, and sometimes fathers and mothers. He agreed with them about everything they said. They talked to him about their loved ones, their families back home, their sweethearts at school, their kids if they had any, and he listened as if he wanted to hear more, was totally interested in their earlier dull lives. They made confessions to him, of past crimes, poured out their guilt feelings concerning some member of their family they had wronged, cried in front of him over some small ambition that was now impossible.

He listened and made the right sounds.

They even spoke to him of their real and imagined illnesses, some of them woman-only problems that they would have found difficult talking to a male doctor about, and he sighed and did his best to calm their fears. They showed him parts of their body, as if he *were* a doctor, and asked him his opinion.

Never were any of the girls molested in any way by Tom, nor did they feel he was interested at all in sexual things. Sensual things, yes. They went to him for a cuddle when they were distressed and he did his best to sooth away the hurts, stroking their hair, holding them in his arms, until they sniffed back the tears, smiled, and said, "Thanks, Tom, you're a real friend," and went about their business again.

As I say, Tom was just *around*, ready to be paid attention to, ready to be attentive, whichever was required.

Even Lavinia was fond of Tom, in a certain way, though she confessed she really had no affection for any creature living in the true sense of the word. Tom was good to have about the house. He kept the girls from leaping occasionally into that hysterical mood which destroyed the harmony needed to maximise business. Tom brought a sort of underlying calm to the house, helped keep the stress at bay, and gave the girls someone to talk to when they were having their periods.

He was useful in other ways too, besides just being there.

One day in the fall, Baby Jane's parents were passing through the town unexpectedly. Baby Jane was one of those rare girls who had chosen the work, rather than had it forced upon her, mainly because she was lazy and had no liking for sex. She didn't see what she did at the house as proper sex: it was just a household chore to her, like lighting a boiler or vacuuming the carpet, except she didn't have to actually do anything except lie there. If she had been married, she would have been expected to *like* the sex, which was out of the question, and she would have been hopeless at faking an orgasm. Married or single she would also have had to do her own housework, or get a job, or both.

Baby Jane sometimes wished she could smoke a cigarette and watch TV while the customer was humping away, to relieve the boredom, but Lavinia wouldn't allow it, so she just did whatever was asked, so long as it didn't involve too much expenditure of energy, and looked forward to the shower afterwards.

This day in the fall she got a call from her mom and dad, who said they would call at her 'lodgings'.

"No, don't do that," said Baby Jane, quickly. "I'll meet you in the Rose Cafe, on the edge of town."

"Why can't we see where you live?" cried her mother.

"Um, I — I want you to meet my boyfriend — my fianceé," she told her mother, "and he can only get away to the cafe for an hour."

"Oh, your *fianceé*," her mom said. "Well, that's different — that's fine. In an hour then."

Baby Jane went racing through the house looking for Bud, who was nowhere to be found. Seizing on Tom she squealed, "Get him dressed up, quick, Kitty — he's got to be my fianceé for an hour."

"Tom? He won't say anything."

"It doesn't matter — I'll think of something."

Spruced up in one of Bud's ill-fitting suits, the pale, slender Tom was marched bewildered to the cafe by Baby Jane and sat in a booth. Baby Jane bought him a glass of milk and cookies, and then her parents arrived, all teeth and wrinkled smiles. There were hugs and kisses and a pumping of hands.

"What do you do, Mr ...?" said Baby Jane's dad, staring hard at Tom.

Tom's head jerked backwards and he looked panicked.

Baby Jane said hastily, "Tom's got laryngitis — it's a sore throat and catching. He doesn't want to give you his germs, Dad, so don't get so close to him."

They ordered English muffins and coffee, and Mom talked animatedly with Baby Jane, occasionally taking a glance at Tom.

Dad said, "What does Tom do?"

"He's a truck driver, Dad — nothing special — but I think he's great." Baby Jane smiled and hooked an arm into Tom's as she said this, and then ruffled his hair a little.

Tom gave her one of his soft smiles.

When they were ready to leave, Baby Jane walked them out to the car, leaving Tom to finish his milk. Baby Jane's dad said quietly to her, "You sure you want to marry this guy, honey? I mean, he's — well — he's kinda *slow*, isn't he?"

"He's fine, Dad — he's a little nervous at meeting you." She gave a tinkling laugh. "And he's not so well, you know, with the sore throat and all."

"Yeah," said Dad, staring back through the window at Tom. "Well, you know what you're doing, sweetie."

They drove away and Baby Jane heaved a sigh of relief.

There were one or two incidents like this, of varying natures, where Tom was able to be used in an emergency. Over the months the girls came to look on Tom as one of those flexible men that women might keep for company around the place, and occasionally was really useful in his way. Mostly though, he just *was*, and nothing more than that. Sometimes the girls were guilty of endowing Tom with talents he didn't have, but that was okay because he never had to prove himself. A whole year he stayed with Kitty and girls at the cat house, then one day something terrible happened, as it always does to innocent creatures who simply just are.

Now, it has been mentioned that Sasha was a junky, but as long as her habit was fed Sasha was a nice person. She had one

other failing however, if it could be so called, in that she was
turned on by gangsters and their crimes. She actually gave a
good performance, and could reach orgasm, if the right man
said the right things while he was with her, even though he
might be a paying customer.

One night Sasha was 'entertaining' a hoodlum by the name
of Jimmy Freeka. Jimmy was a mobster from the city, swiftly
rising in the hierarchy of his particular Family, and while he was
with Sasha he would tell her about the guys he had killed or
maimed, going into detail concerning weapons, raw
amputations, broken bones, and the death rattles of victims. He
himself was turned on by his own confessions to her, while
Sasha drank it all in, getting hotter by the minute, until the pair
of them were high on blood and death, and going into ecstatic
convulsions in a place where sex was normally a dry and
tasteless activity.

This particular night, Jimmy was saying to Sasha, as he
stroked her between the legs with his left hand, " ... so this guy,
Stark — Asa Stark his name was — you must remember the
papers — it was all over the headlines — I waited for him at the
back of his club — The Blue Box — Sal Maccino's joint — with
one of those ice axes mountain climbers use."

"Oh God," whispered Sasha, closing her eyes and finally
guiding him in, "what happened?"

"Like I said, I waited — uhhh — I — uhh, this is good, baby
— I waited with this axe thing with a spike on top — that's
soooo good — yeah, and when he come out of the club, I steps
up to him and I says, *Hey,* just that, *Hey,* and I drove the fuckin'
spike through his left eye — aagghhhh."

"Yes, yes, *yes, yes,*" screamed Sasha.

"He sorta jumped a little — like someone had put an electric
wire to his crotch — and I said, *Die you faggot* — and-he-sorta-
crumpled-like-he-was-made-of-aaaahhhhhhhhggoddddddd."

Sasha then made a sound which was not often heard for real
in a brothel and subsided into delicious shudders.

When they had finished, Jimmy Freeka rolled over onto his
back and caught sight of someone standing in the doorway of
the room, quietly. Jimmy quickly reached for his gun, which as

always was under the pillow, but Sasha said, "No Jimmy, it's only Tom. Go away Tom …"

"How long you been standin' there?" Jimmy asked, screwing his eyes up.

Tom didn't answer. He just left the room.

Jimmy lay back and smoked a cigarette after that, not saying anything more to Sasha, but later he went and had a word with Lavinia.

"That guy, Tom. He's got to go — permanently."

"What?" said Lavinia, looking surprised. "Tom?"

"Yeah."

"I'll send him away, on the next train going north," said Lavinia.

"No trains — he don't go nowhere. He stays here, but he don't do no more breathing," said Jimmy, "otherwise this place will be ashes, you understand me? You know who I am. You know the kind of people I work for. If you don't do it, we will, and it might be messy. This nice rug here might get messed. Okay?"

"Hey, Jimmy," said Lavinia, quietly, "you don't want to do this — Tom's a pussy cat. He scared of his own shadow. Besides, he doesn't talk to anyone except Kitty. Why don't you let it go, eh, Jimmy? I can make it worth your while."

Jimmy Freeka lowered his eyes and stared at a spot just two feet away from his left foot: a sure sign that he was angry.

"Do it," was all he said.

Late that night Lavinia called all the girls together, except Kitty who was sent on an errand, and told them what they had to do. She wanted them all to be implicated. She believed it was safer that way, with no secrets to hide from each other. There were protests of course, and even some vehement threats against Jimmy, but eventually the girls realised that Lavinia had no choice. Jimmy's organisation was very powerful and none of the girls wanted to be crippled or disfigured. With heavy hearts they agreed that nothing could save Tom and that it was best done quietly and painlessly, for everyone else's sake as well as his own.

Lavinia, not trusting any of the others to do the job properly,

mixed the powder in the warm milk and took it to Tom herself.
Tom was asleep on the pool table. She woke him and gave him
the concoction, smiling sadly as she watched him drink it. He
dozed for a while after that. A little while later Tom stirred and
coughed up something onto the green baize, which distressed
him, but Lavinia who was waiting nearby said it could easily be
removed with a little kitchen cleanser and some strong rubbing,
without balding the table top too much. Tom nodded and lay his
head back down.

Tom fell asleep again, shortly afterwards, forever.

Lavinia stayed by the body for a whole hour and though she
didn't cry a single tear, anyone who knew her would have been
shocked by the compassion in her eyes.

Bud took the body and drove across town with it, placing it
amongst some restaurant trash cans around which he knew rat
poison had been laid.

Baby Jane rang her parents and told them in a subdued and
solemn voice, not altogether faked, that Tom had died at the
wheel of his truck of a massive brain haemorrhage.

"The truck left the highway and went seven miles out into
the desert," she said, elaborating on the scenario. "They found
him the next day. My — my picture was stuck to the
dashboard."

Her parents said they were shocked, but when her dad spoke
to her a little later she detected some relief in his tone as he said,
"I knew there was something the matter with that boy the
minute I saw him."

Kitty was absolutely distraught when she heard that Tom had
died of eating poisoned food and wept uncontrollably. "He was
such a sweet man," she said. "The nicest man I've ever met …"
They all agreed with her, helped wipe away the running mascara,
gave her hugs, and Sasha went out and bought her a canary, the
only kind of pet Lavinia would allow in the establishment.

Tom was buried in a pauper's grave in the Baptist burial
ground south of the town. No one knew whether he was a
Baptist or not, but the area was strongly Roman Catholic and
the Baptists needed corpses to fill their sparsely populated
graveyard, so they took Tom as one of their own. It made them

feel they were gaining ground on their rivals.

Kitty visited the grave quite often at first, leaving small bunches of flowers, but gradually her visits grew less. A year is a long time in the boring, slow life of a whore, and Kitty eventually made excuses not to go, and finally stopped the trips all together. When a travelling salesman asked about Tom, on one of his regular visits, Sasha said dreamily, "Poor Tom, he had to be put down."

"What?" said the salesman, caught in mid-penetration.

"Nothing," replied Sasha, suddenly aware of her incaution, "you know these strays — they come and go."

"Yeah, I suppose so," grunted the salesman, and then concentrated on applying himself to the work in hand, in order to get his money's worth before his time ran out.

Exactly a year and a day after Lavinia had been ordered to put Tom to sleep, Jimmy Freeka was at a funeral, paying his final respects to the memory of a rival mobster he had gunned down a week earlier. On his way back to his car he walked over Tom's grave, not even looking down to see who was buried there, and kicked over a saucer of Kitty's milk-white daisy-heads.

A few moments later, while Jimmy was crossing the street outside the cemetery, a small lithe creature as dark and anonymous as a shadow darted across the highway. The shadow ran on through Jimmy's legs, causing him to falter indecisively in front of a speeding truck. The truck driver seemed to swerve his vehicle instinctively, but not to avoid the fallen man. It seemed to deliberately run him down.

The vehicle struck the hoodlum, throwing him up into the air like a mangy dog hit by a train.

Jimmy left the world in great pain on his way to the hospital and was pronounced DOA.

It was a hit and run: the truck did not stop.

There was one witness to the accident, a man walking home from work. The witness could not recall the registration on the license plate, but said the driver was wearing a black baseball cap with a yellow peak. The cap bore a company logo: a single three-letter word in yellow diamond, on the front.

"And what was that word?" asked the officer.

"C-A-T," replied the witness.

HARDBOILED STIFF
by Michael Hemmingson

I
"Who the fuck killed me?"

... and then I woke up. I couldn't breathe. It was, in retrospect, the most godawful feeling I ever had and God had nothing to do with it. I didn't know where the hell I was. Mud, thick and wet like greasy shit, filled my mouth and it didn't taste like anything really; it was slimy and going down my throat — *I couldn't scream, I could not fucking scream and that was the one thing I wanted to do most of all.*

I was under the earth.

I reached out and broke free — my fist felt air and the storm. It was raining hard. The rain was making the dirt above me into mud.

I pulled myself up, I climbed out.

The grave I was in was shallow, dug in haste.

I had no idea how I got there.

I wasn't even sure who I was — my name, my profession; the year, what city I was in.

I was in a dark and desolate place. Thunder rolled across the sky and the rain came down harder. I spit out the mud from my mouth, blew it out of my nose, opened my mouth to the dark and stormy sky and drank the rain.

I was so goddamn thirsty.

I wore a gray and rumpled suit, torn here and there; my shirt was untucked and my thin black tie loosened. I didn't have any shoes on. I thought: They bury the dead barefoot.

But I wasn't dead.

Whoever put me in the grave fucked up.

And I was going to *fuck them up.*

I'm a Scorpio, I like revenge.

Funny: that's all I knew about myself: my zodiac sign and that I was, or had been, the unforgiving sort.

I touched my chest and felt the bullet holes. I'd been shot twice, and I kind of remembered *that.* Yes, I'd been shot in the chest, in the heart, but I didn't know who did it, or why.

I stuck my finger into the bullet holes. No blood.

Any other time, that'd be funny.

I began to walk.

The one question in my mind, the only thing that was driving me to move through this storm and the night, was: Who killed me?

Who the fuck killed me, and how the heck did I come back to life?

***

I found the road and the road looked familiar. I knew I had to walk west, that would get me somewhere. I walked with my bare feet and stared at the ground. The rainstorm subsided and became a manageable drizzle. It was cold but I didn't feel cold. I didn't feel much. I noticed light. I looked up. Two high beams. A car was approaching. The light hurt my eyes as the car got closer. I moved, slowly (my back somewhat at a hunch, my feet dragging) to the other side of the road and put my thumb out.

I could only imagine how I looked. *How I smelled.* Nobody in his or her right mind would give a horrid, ungainly fellow like me a lift.

But it was worth a try.

So I put my thumb out.

The car was a nice big Buick with tail fins. It stopped. The window rolled down. The man driving was in his fifties, wore a Hawaiian shirt and polyester pants. He took one glance at me and said: "Holy shit."

"I know," I said, "listen —"

He shook his head with apparent disgust, was about to gun it. Something took me over — something vile and ancient; something revolting and, in a grand and unspeakable way, *pure.* I took hold of the door handle and pulled. The door was locked; I had incredible strength and *knew* I had this powerful thing inside me — or the burning call for what I did next; it gave me the superhuman capacity to break the lock and literally yank the door off and toss the door aside, into the air, like it was cardboard.

So this is what happened: I grabbed the man by the collar of his Hawaiian shirt — complimented him on the fabric — then snapped his neck like a straw, bashed his skull in half a dozen times onto the hood of his Buick until his head was split open and his brains were exposed; then I clamped my mouth down onto his brains and had myself a feast.

Oh, it was sick and vile and somewhere in the back of my own brain (if I even had one now) I was telling myself to stop — *but I could not stop.* I relished the taste of the blood and skull meat ... and the more I ate, the better I felt.

It was the only thing that mattered in the universe, in that very crucial moment: that I eat a human brain and shudder in the ecstasy and tasty delight of it all.

There was something wrong with me, sure, but I didn't give a fuck.

II
"The Gideon Private Investigation Agency"

I drove the Buick downtown. Signs told me that I was in Miami, Florida. Dade County. Oh yes, that rang a bell all right. There was a wallet in my jacket pocket; at a stop sign, I looked in it. $33 in wrinkled, wet tens and ones and a Florida Driver's License. Arthur Laurence Gideon. DOB: 11-15-33. I also had a private investigator's license, with a business address. I knew where that place was, where my office was. *My office.* I knew who I was now; I just didn't know who the fuck killed me.

I knew that it was October in 1966. I was 33-years-old and would be 34 next month. I'd been married ten years ago, when I lived in San Diego; my young wife had died of cancer.

I lived alone, I was alone, and I was a gumshoe in Miami.

That's all I could recall …

I parked the Buick in front of the building where I had my office. It was starting to rain hard again.

I had keys in my pants pocket. The light was on in my office, which was located at the back end of the third floor.

I went inside.

A woman's voice — a yelp, a small scream, one gasp —

"*Arty?!?*"

"Who goes there?" I said.

"Who do you *think?*"

She was a curvy, voluptuous brunette with short-cropped hair and large, pointed breasts in a very *very* tight white blouse and a *very* very tight black skirt cut two-inches above the knee, in black stockings and black three-inch pumps. She wore black-rimmed glasses and bright red lipstick. It took me a few seconds, but I remembered who she was.

"Ms. Melfile," I said with a sigh.

Her name was Lissa Melfile and she was my secretary, had been for the past eighteen months.

"Arty," she said. "I mean, Mr. Gideon. Oh gosh."

"What?"

"Nothing."

"Tell me."

"I — I wasn't expecting you."

"Why are you looking at me like that?" I asked.

"I —"

"*Tell me.*"

"You look *awful.*"

I said, "I feel awful."

"I wasn't," she started to say, and began to cry.

I glanced at the wall clock. "It's three in the morning. What are you doing here at this hour?"

"Waiting for you, of course," she said. "I've been worried."

"How long have I been gone?"

She looked at me with watery eyes like she figured I was nuts.

"*How long?*" I said.

"Three days," she replied softly.

"I don't remember the last three days," I said, "or even the last three weeks, or three months. My memory ... has some ... gaps."

I hoped I looked as confused as I felt.

"Maybe you're missing some of your, uh, memory," and she was looking at my head when she told me this, and cried more.

I said: "What is it? Why are you —"

"Go look in the mirror, Mr. Gideon."

I went into the bathroom and turned on the light. Let's just say that I was not prepared for what I saw in the mirror above the basin ...

I almost screamed but did not. A man does not scream like a little girl when he's in his office and his secretary is near.

Not only was I pasty pale with dark circles under my yellow eyes, not only did I have two bullet holes in my chest and blood and mud and who-knows-what-else all over my suit and skin, but I was missing half the left side of my head and my brain matter was exposed.

Not only that my left eye was dangling out of the socket. I popped it back in.

"Aw, shit," I whispered.

Plus I was barefoot!

***

I told my secretary to please stop crying and she nodded. I told her to sit down and she sat in the chair in front of my big expensive oak desk. I remembered paying a lot of money for this desk — I always wanted such a desk and the day I could afford it, I went and got it. Well, at least I remembered *something*. Little things were coming back, like torn parts of blurry photographs. I felt like drinking booze, for some goddamn reason, and I knew I had the stuff — right in the big desk. I opened a drawer and found a half-full bottle of Maker's Mark and a few little paper cups.

"Join me?" I said.

"Always," Lissa Melfile said.

She sat and crossed her long legs; I looked at her legs and knew I should be feeling something — a distant stir that had to be desire, sex.

And I felt nothing.

Ms. Melfile sipped at her cup and coughed like she wasn't used to the burn of alcohol. "That always hits the spot," she said, and I remembered suddenly that she seldom drank.

I drank and again I felt nothing — not the singe, not the warmth, not the buzz in the head that makes people want to drink more and more.

"What happened to you, Mr. Gideon?" she asked.

"Do you call me by my first name, or 'Mr. Gideon'?"

She blushed. "Depends. Both."

"Depends on what?"

"Oh," she said and looked away.

"Are we sleeping together?"

"I could be insulted by a remark like that. I *should* be."

"I'm sorry."

"I understand — it's a memory thing."

"Well?"

"We were, for a short while …"

"But?"

"But it wasn't feeling like the right thing to do," she said. "I mean, I work for you. We have that employer-employee relationship. You said —"

"How goddamn typical for a private eye to be slipping the sausage to his secretary."

"Yes! That's what you said! And —"

I sat back in my chair and said: "I hate being a cliché."

"*Yes*, that's what you — you remember now?"

"No. But I figure that's what I'd say. It's what I'm thinking … right now."

"It was both of us," she said. "I didn't … well, Arty, if I can call you that, Mr. Gideon … I often wonder about your heart."

I looked at the holes in my chest.

She said: "Most of the time it's like you don't have any feelings in you. Like you don't have any emotions. I know you gotta be tough in this business, but when you're with a lady in the bedroom, a man has to drop the hardboiled act … unless it's not an act."

I nodded.

"You know what I mean?"

"No," I said, "but I'm beginning to hark back to a night or two that we fucked."

"Sometimes you can be a real *bastard*, Mr. Gideon!"

"I know."

"But that's okay," she said. "Most people are bastards."

"I still don't recollect a whole lot."

"So you don't know how — you got like you are?"

"No."

"Maybe it'll come back."

"Do you know what I was doing? What case I was on?"

"I should hope so," she said with a smile, "or else I'd be a very bad secretary. You were on a missing persons case — some runaway girl, came from a rich family. But don't they all?"

"I was about to say that."

"Of course you were."

We smiled at each other. I wondered how gory my smile looked; hers was very pretty.

Pretty. Yes. She was. I was feeling something down there, that thing I called my prick.

"Was I making any progress?" I asked.

"You never really tell me the details of your cases. I write your reports when you give them to me, handle your correspondence and invoices ..."

I nodded.

"Arty?"

"Yes."

"You look like you're dead."

"Yeah," I said, "I do."

"I mean, the wounds on you ..."

"Ain't pretty, is it," I said.

"You *should* be dead."

"I think I am."

"I was afraid something like that happened, like your check got cashed."

But she was looking at my face with too much interest for me to believe she had any fear.

I said: "What's the girl's name? The one I'm looking for?"

"Jenna Rush. Her father is Samuel Rush."

"He's rich? A big wig?"

"*Senator* Rush," she said. "The Rushes go back to the plantation days. Old money."

"A Senator?"

"Our very own Republican."

"Hmmm," I hmmmed. "Do I usually take cases for government officials?"

"Mr. Gideon," she said, "you take *any* case, as long as the money is green and it isn't counterfeit."

III
"Weird sex with a secret necrophile"

Obviously what I had to do was backtrack; I'd need to call on the Senator, find out just what, exactly, he sent me on. Ms. Melfile said I didn't have any other cases pending, so somewhere along in my sleuthing to find the missing girl I died and came back to life and had a desire to eat human brains.

It was a good thing I gobbled down the brains of that guy in the Buick and I was satiated on the matter, for now; or else I may have cracked open my secretary's skull and feasted on her mind. Instead, I kept looking at her pointy breasts and legs and feeling some other kind of want.

"What I really need to do is call Senator Rush," I said out loud, and reached for the phone.

"At *this* uncivilized hour?" Ms. Melfile said.

I put the phone down. "Of course. It can wait till later."

She yawned.

"Maybe I should get some rest," I said, "go to bed."

"That would be a good idea."

"I have an apartment? A home? Or do I sleep here on the couch?"

"You have a bungalow by the beach. It's very nice."

"Do you have a car? I need a ride ... home."

"Yes. What happened to your vehicle?"

"I don't know. I came here in a stolen Buick."

"*Stolen?*"

"Borrowed," I said.

"Oh Arty," she said.

"What," I said, "do I do this often?"

She sighed and said: "Let's go, I'll drive you home."

***

She had a VW Bug. I felt cramped inside but couldn't complain, she was concerned for me and that was an alien feeling. I kept looking at Ms. Melfile's pleasing-to-the-eye (even if I had one that kept popping out) legs. She drove a few miles toward the beach, to a stretch of beach bungalows that looked pricey and cozy. Parked in front of one and said: "This is your bachelor pad, Mr. Gideon."

"Shit." I felt through my pockets. "I don't have any keys."

"I know where you keep your spare."

She walked and I followed and the way she moved her curvaceous hips and amble rump, things *were* going on inside me. At least there was some sensation returning to the body — but that could work against me: I might feel the pain that should be accompanying my wounds.

We stood at the front entrance of the bungalow.

She bent down and *that* did it for me — I had to fuck her. She turned and looked at me and her eyes said she wanted to be fucked. This was not wishful thinking, I knew that look if I knew only one thing in the world. "Here is your spare," she said, reaching under a flowerpot and producing a silver key.

"Yes," I said, "of course," but my thoughts were on her ass.

She straightened and opened the door and we went inside. She turned on the light and asked: "Does it look familiar?"

"I'm sure it will."

"Well, this is home sweet home."

"And where do you live?"

"Not too far away," she said, glancing at me with that *look* again.

"Ms. Melfile," I said, pulling at my tie, "I thank you for the ride and your assistance; I'm going to have to apologize in advance for what I'm about to do."

"Oh," she said, touching her chest, "are you going to turn me into a zombie?"

"A *what?*"

"A *zombie.* That's what you are."

"I don't know what I am," I said, "but only vampires and werewolves can turn people into —"

"I think zombies can too," she said.

"Well, that's not what I had in ..."

"What were you ... ?"

I was looking at her knockers and feeling a whole lot of lust. She said: "Oh."

"I know I'm an miserly sight — I stink of death and violence and who-knows-what, so I'm telling you now that I'm sorry for what I'm about to do."

"Please," she told me, "just get it over with." She softly smiled. "Just do what you have to do," she said.

I lunged like a Bengal tiger on its prey and she did not fight me. She kissed me back. She pulled at my clothes. She let me take off her blouse and bra and play with those wonderful tits in my big decaying hands.

"I want your ass," I said.

"Oh, Mr. Gideon, you can have *every* part of my body!"

***

"You don't mind?" I asked.

"Not at all," she said.

"I thought I was going to have to ravish and rape you," I said.

"Ravish me all you want, Arty," she said, "rape me any way you wish. I just want you to take me and ... and ..."

***

We fucked and my eye kept popping out and small pieces of me flung off when we got especially vigorous. You'd think I'd be embarrassed but if she didn't care, why the hell should I? Like the song says: we were having a grand old time.

***

"I have a confession to make," she said.

"I'm listening."

"I like dead people."

"I know that."

"I don't mean just now," she said, "always."

"Oh?"

"Before I worked for you, I had a job at a mortuary. I was fired."

"Why?"

"I was caught fucking a dead body."

"I bet he wasn't as responsive as me."

"I can't say that he was," she winked, "but I'll never be able to get a job at another mortuary or morgue again."

"So you've always been this way?" I asked.

"My secret desire," she said, "I'm what you call a necrophile."

"Yesterday I would have found that perverse," I said, "but now ... I find it very nice."

"The sex was *nice.*"

"Nice? It was fucking *great.*"

"I love fucking a man who is dead; you don't know how satisfied I feel right now, Arty."

"I'm feeling pretty good myself, girl."

"Maybe this is the start of something ... special."

Maybe.

Who knows.

I lived day-to-day like any other goddamn gumshoe, I could do the same as a zombie.

"Tell me," I said, "how long have you been into screwing the dead?"

"It all began when my high school sweetheart died," she said, looking sad in the bedroom with me as the sun started to rise outside. "I was fifteen and he was sixteen and oh we were in love so much. We never went all the way but he would put his fingers inside me and I would suck on his penis and I couldn't wait for the day until we were married and we could have sex like a man and a wife. I came from a good Catholic family, you understand, and while I did certain things, I wasn't about to have pre-marital intercourse. Anyway, one day we were walking home from school, holding hands, and then he was trying to be — he wanted — I don't know *what* he was doing, he was playing around, but he let go of my hand and he said, 'Watch how fast I can run!' He was on the track team, you understand. Anyway, he ran into the street and the garbage truck was coming down the way really fast and the truck hit my sweetheart and killed him right there on the spot. His twisted, broken body was on the street — neck, legs and arms completely broken … and he had this silly grin on his face, like he was smiling at me. I went to him, I went to his dead body, I held him in my arms, I was prepared to cry and scream like any girl who has just lost her love would, like Juliet, but I didn't. What I felt was … excitement. My body was on fire with strange pleasure and my crotch was so very wet and I kept having orgasm after orgasm until the ambulance arrived and they had to pry me away from his body. But it was not grief that made me want to be with his body — it was delight. Did I think this odd you ask? Yes. Yes, it was quite odd and — wicked. But every time I thought of him — that way: dead — my vagina started to spasm. Oh, you should have *seen* me at the funeral, I had to pretend I was crying and horrified, but I was secretly having many orgasms, just looking at his pale and still form in the casket. Then I would masturbate in bed, late at night in the dark, thinking about him. I still do."

Silence.

"Arty?"

Her breathing was hard, her breath rancid from having the taste of my cock on her tongue.

"Mr. Gideon," she said, "what do you make of my life story?"

"That," I said, "is a weird tale, Ms. Melfile."

"Oh, Arty," she said, kissing me, "shut up and let's make love one more time and then we can sleep in each other's arms."

***

She slept, but I could not. I wasn't tired in the least. I had no idea if the dead were capable of sleeping — do they need it? She lightly snored as she snuggled against me and this was all right, this was nice.

I closed my eyes and tried to rest or sleep —
But like a car slamming into me, it all came back —
A flood of images —
The dead — so many of them —
The dead like me —
And naked young people fucking —
They were all laughing —
At me —
Laughing and hurting —
— me.
Me.
I screamed.
I sat up and screamed.

"Arty," Lissa Melfile said, her hand on my back, "Arty, what is it?"

I was shaking.

"I remember everything now," I said.

IV
"Now I know what happened to me"

It went like this:

A tall leggy blonde in an expensive pale blue woman's suit and matching pill box hat waltzed into my office one day and asked if I was available for hire.

Don't these things always start with such a leggy blonde?

Nevertheless, I said: "What's the job?"

"Someone's missing."

"Isn't somebody always missing?"

"Do you want the job or not?" she asked with a huff.

"Sure," I said, "tell me about it."

"You need to come with me then."

"Why can't you tell me about it here?"

"I'm not the one who has anything to tell," she said, "it's my employer."

"Who is?"

"Sam Rush."

"As in — ?"

"Senator Rush."

"Ah, *that* Senator Rush."

"So you know him."

"I know *of* him. Who doesn't around here? Hasn't he done enough to fuck up the south Florida economy?"

"His daughter is missing."

"I'm sorry to hear that."

"He'll tell you more, if you take the job."

"I'm willing to listen to what he has to say," I said, my feelings going out for a worried father but not for a rich politician, "and I'm willing to help if I can."

"Good. Let's go."

There was a car and driver waiting outside.

"Nice," I said.

"Yes, isn't it."

I scrutinized her legs and ass as she got into the car.

I said: "Nice."

She gave me a look.

"Help yourself to the wet bar," she said with a sigh.

I did.

"You?" I said.

"I don't drink during working hours," she said.

As we drove, I asked her name. We were sitting across from each other.

"Jill," she said. "Listen, Mr. Gideon, let me give you three points of advice before you meet the Senator: (1) don't have a smart mouth with him, (2) don't say anything about the economy to him and (3) don't ogle my body parts in front of him — it'll piss him off and he's a man you do *not* want to piss off."

"Why, Jill? You his girlfriend?"

"I'm one of his top aides."

"One?"

"*The,*" she said.

"But you're screwing the man," I said.

"That's none of your business."

"And what does his wife do? She heads the local chapter of the Red Cross, right?"

"Mr. Gideon," she said, "in this matter, I expect you to be a civilized, discreet professional."

I said: "My sincere hope, Jill, is that I do not disappoint you."

"Believe me," she said, "if it was my decision and choice, you wouldn't be riding with me anywhere."

The car went to the land of the wealthy, to the one hundred and fifty acre Rush Estate and its twenty-room mansion.

I whistled.

"Nice, yes?" Jill said.

"I'll never know, baby."

***

The Senator was waiting for me in his study. He looked like he hadn't slept for a few days. He appeared worried and I felt for the weight the man must have been carrying.

He was staring out one of the big windows, holding a stiff drink in his hand.

"Please, sir, sit down," he said.

I sat.

"Would you like some gin? Bourbon? Whiskey? Vodka?"

"I had two drinks on the ride here. My limit is two during working hours," I lied.

He smiled, but it was a sad smile.

"Mr. Rush," I said, "I understand you have a problem and maybe I can help."

"I hope you can help. I asked around: who's the best P.I. to hire? Your name came up several times."

"Is that good or bad?"

"You tell me."

"Let's say it's good."

"Good," he said, and sat down at his desk. "My daughter is missing."

"So I was told."

"Were you told anything else?"

"That's all Jill said."

"Jill is a good woman."

"So I gather."

"You 'gather'?"

"She seems good," I said, "a top aide."

"*The* top aide."

"So she said."

"And *great* in the sack." He grinned.

"I imagine."

"You don't have to imagine. I can arrange a meeting, in a hotel room. Would you like to fuck her? She's a good fuck."

"Well," I said, not knowing what to say to that.

"I tell you what," said the Senator, "you find my little girl, Jill's pussy will be a bonus."

"Tell me about your daughter."

"Her name is Jenna — Jennifer, but she goes by Jenna. Named after her sacred grandmother, my saintly mother. Jenna is thirteen and she has run away from home."

"How long has she — ?"

"Two and a half weeks now."

"You call the cops?"

"Informally," he said. "I don't want this to leak to the press. It wouldn't be good."

"It might help find her."

"It would only look bad. Jenna was hanging out — with a bad crowd. You know this stuff with the kids now — all this *hippie* nonsense."

"I've heard about it," I said. "I've been seeing the hippies around."

"Drugs and free love and radical politics," he said with distaste. "Long hair and unwashed bodies and — *free love.*"

"Free love."

"Do you know what that is?"

"Not really."

"Indiscriminate sex," he said. "And sex with children. Jenna is only thirteen."

"Didn't you tell her to stay away from that riffraff?" I asked him.

"I tried, oh I tried. I lectured, I grounded her. This is what drove her to run away. The classic western culture parent-child situation of misunderstanding: she leaves home. Leaves a note: 'It's time for me to split, Daddy-o.' Can you believe that? What does 'split' mean? Where does she come off referring to me as 'Daddy-o'?"

"Kids these days," and I rolled my eyes for effect.

"Tell me about it," he said. "So you can understand my delicate problem, sir. Not only am I a member of the sacred body of the American Senate, there is the family name that goes back many generations in these parts."

"Yes."

"And if this were to get into the press — Rush Family daughter running around with unwashed hippies and taking that LSD stuff and engaging in 'free love' …"

"I understand."

"I believe you do." He opened the drawer in front of his desk and brought out some Polaroid pictures. "This is Jenna."

I looked at them.

"Pretty girl," I said.

I wanted to say *sexy*, for a thirteen-year-old, but that's not the sort of comment a grown man makes in front of a teenage girl's father.

"Will you find her for me?" asked the Senator. "Will you take the case?"

"I'll do my best," I said. "But where do I start?"

"That's your job, sir, not mine."

***

Rush gave me a handsome retainer, five times what I normally charge. I was feeling happy and wanted to celebrate. Ms. Melfile was at the office when I was taken back in the car (without Jill, and I had two more drinks). I reached behind my secretary and squeezed her big tits and whispered into her ears: "I got some good dough, baby, and I think we should go out and have a night."

"Arty," she said, pushing me away, "don't."

"What is it?"

"You know ..."

"Know what?"

"Like I said last night, we can't do this anymore. *I* can't. It's just not in me, and it's not right."

"Right," I said with a heavy, overdramatic sigh, moving away from her, giving her space. "Well, guess who I'm looking for?"

"Who?"

"A lost little rich girl."

"Another one?"

"She's very young."

"They keep getting younger. I don't even *remember* being a young girl." At first I thought Ms. Melfile was being facetious, but I noticed how sad her face looked.

"She ran off with hippies," I said.

"*Hippies?*"

"Yeah."

"She *is* lost."

***

... and so I went to South Beach and did the footwork: showing the Rush girl's photo around to every hippie-looking person I spotted and could uncover, either alone or in groups, high and sober, coherent or, as they said, "spaced-out."

Most of them said they'd never seen her, but I knew they were lying; they just didn't trust me.

"You a cop, man?"

I said: "No."

"You look like a cop, man."

"I'm a private eye, man."

"Far out, man."

"So you haven't seen this girl?"

"No, man, never seen her."

Right.

"You a cop, man?" a girl who was fifteen and half-naked on the beach asked me, shading the sun from her eyes with a little hand.

"No," I said.

"You look square."

"I'm not."

"You *look* it."

"Well, I'm *not.*"

"You wanna drop acid with us, man?"

"Are you sure you haven't seen this girl?" I said.

"I don't know, man, you see a lot of people but it's hard to really remember the faces, you know what I mean?"

But there was also this:

"Yeah, she used to hang around here, but haven't seen her in weeks."

"Oh yeah, she went by the name of, uh, Bright Sunshine, I think, I only met her once."

"No, she said her name was Wallflower."

"No, it was Daisy."

"Oh yeah, I fucked that little girl. Man, she was high that night. Man, that pussy was some *tight* pussy."

"She sucked my dick *twice* for beer and weed."

"I think she has a pimp, man."

"She goes to school with my little sister. Is that weird or *what?*"

"I haven't seen her in a month."

"I haven't seen her in *days.*"

"I don't know where she crashes, man."

***

... and I was going to my car when a skinny, smelly hippie fellow with B.O. and dirty long blonde hair came up to me and said: "Hey, man, $10 and I'll tell you where you can find her. Wallflower."

"How do I know your information is good?"

He shrugged. "Take it or leave it."

I got out my wallet and gave him two fives.

He gave me an address and an apartment number.

"That's where she's staying?" I asked.

"*No,* man," he said, "that's where a wild party is happenin' tonight."

"Wild?"

"Party. You know, lots of drugs and sex. We call them 'love-ins'."

"Yeah?"

"Yeah, and she'll be there."

"How do you know?"

"She goes to *every* orgy in town, man."

"You know she's thirteen?"

"Yeah that's why she's popular. I seen twelve-year-old chicks at some of these orgies, man. Wild, huh?"

"Wild," I said.

***

... and I went, that night, to the address and the apartment number. It was in a shitty part of town. There was loud music and a lot of moaning inside. I knocked and knocked on the door and was about ready to break it down or climb through the window when it opened. A naked woman in her 20s stood there; she was rail thin with frizzy red hair, glassy eyes, and a thick bush of dark pubic hair.

"Look at you," she said.

"Hello," I said.

"Trippy," she said, "look at you in the suit, man!"

Two more naked girls joined her and they glared at me up and down with silly grins on their pussies — uh, faces.

"Wild," one said.

"Who are you?" the other said.

"I'm looking for a girl," I said.

One said, "Well you came to the right place," and all three of them grabbed me and pulled me inside.

The room was thick with marijuana smoke and empty beers

bottles lined the walls. What can I say about the floor? It was a sea of human flesh; it was, for all intents and purposes, a Mongolian Clusterfuck. I guess I *was* square, I'd never been to anything like this — I'd heard about such things but didn't believe they were true. But here it all was, before me: dozens of naked men and women of all ages fucking and sucking and moaning and groaning. I don't have to describe what it all smelled like, even the pot smoke didn't cover that smell, a smell that I admit turned me on.

The three girls who pulled me inside were pulling off my clothes; they were saying, "C'mon, baby, let's get it on," and kissing me and grabbing me. I was waving Jenna Rush's photo about when I saw the girl, right in the middle of the orgy; all she wore were a pair of white panties and moccasin boots, her hair done in braids. She was marvelously tanned from head to toe and she had men taking her from both ends. Both were in their forties and had long, thick beards and smiling at one another as they did the Senator's daughter.

I called out her name.

The music was too loud.

"What is this noise?"

"It's the Airplane!" one of the girls said.

I screamed, "JENNA! JENNA RUSH! YOUR DADDY IS LOOKING FOR YOU!"

All the fucking stopped and there were many eyes on me.

The music played on —

When the truth is gone ...

"JENNA RUSH!" I yelled.

"Oh shit!" the girl shrieked, pushing the two men and their hard penises away.

"JENNA! COME HERE!"

"*Fuck you, pig!*" she said, grabbing a flower print dress from the floor and running past me.

I went after her.

"*Hey!*" said the naked women. "*Come back! You don't want her, she's a little girl. We're women. We know how to fuck!*"

As much as I wanted to stay, I had a job to do.

Jenna slipped on her flower print dress as she ran.

"Come back!"

"TELL MY DADDY TO GO TO FUCKING HELL, MAN!"

We were running down the street, toward the beach.

That's when some guys in leather jackets grabbed me.

One of them hit me in the back of the head.

They also grabbed Jenna.

"Is this her?"

"It's her."

"What the," I said.

These guys, something was wrong with them — they had no faces. Well, their faces were skulls with rotting drooping flesh and eyeballs dangling from the sockets; plus they were slouched and moved about in a funny manner, like their bodies were stiff.

"What the fuck," I said.

I was hit on the head again and, as the story often goes, everything went black ...

***

... and I came to, back inside the apartment where the orgy was going on, but now it was no longer a "love in" with all the many sounds of pleasure, it was a slaughter house of madness and there were many screams of pain, fear, and death. The guys in leather jackets, these guys with skulls for faces, five of them in all, were killing naked men and women left and right, smashing their heads open and feasting on their brains, smearing blood all over their rotting flesh and laughing. A sixth one, who seemed to be the leader and was the tallest, held Jenna Rush by both of her arms; he watched and took glee in this sickness. Jenna tried to get free but she was too small and weak. She looked at me with terror, and then I blacked out again ...

***

... and came to out in the middle of nowhere. A storm had rolled in and it was beginning to rain, thunder in the sky. Two of the skull faces were digging a hole in the ground. Jenna Rush was sitting on the ground, her arms tied behind her by rope. The leader was pointing a revolver at me.

"You were in the wrong place at the wrong time," he said.

"Who are you?" I coughed, rubbing the back of my head and feeling the two large bumps there.

"People call me The Power," he said. "My Momma calls me Stevie."

"Let her go," I said. "Let us both go, and you won't have any trouble."

"Trouble?" he laughed, and his five cohorts laughed with him. "We *are* trouble, my man. I should change my name from The Power to The Trouble from Hell."

"Let the girl go."

"Can't do that."

"Do you know who she *is?* Who her goddamn *father* is?"

The Power seemed to grin, if a skull can do that. "Yes," he informed me, "I do."

Then he shot me: two bullets in the chest.

I looked at the bullet holes, and the blood coming out.

"Oh shit," I said.

"You'll be dead soon, don't worry. Would you like one in the head? Then we'll bury you nice and comfy."

"Hey, Power, let's make him one of us," said one of his crew.

"Yeah," said another, "I bet his brains taste reeeeeeeaaaallll gooooooood."

"What?" said The Power. "You zombies didn't get enough at the party?"

"There can never be enough," all five said.

"True," said The Power. "Well," he said to me, "you'll come in handy, I think. When you rise from your grave, you'll deliver a message to Senator Rush. A very important message. You'll tell him The Power Platoon has come home to roost."

The other five converged on me as I lay dying from the gun shot wounds. They smashed my face in, broke my head open and began to greedily eat ...

The last thing I remembered hearing was The Power saying: "Take off his shoes and socks. We bury the dead barefoot, remember?"

V
" ... "

... and then I woke up. I couldn't breathe —

VI
"The truth about the zombies"

"I can't breathe," I said, coughing.

"It's okay," Ms. Melfile was saying, touching my back, "you're just having a flashback."

I'd told her everything as it came back to me —

I stood up.

"This is ridiculous," I said, "if I'm dead, how can I be breathing? *Do* the dead breathe?"

"You're dead, but you're not *really* ... "

"I don't like being like this. Is there a cure?"

"I don't know," Ms. Melfile said. "But I like you this way. You know? I really do."

"Obviously what I have to do is find The Power and rescue the Senator's daughter."

"How will you do that?"

"I'll go back to where this all started, where that party was."

"Some party!"

"Wait," I said, scratching my skull, the hair and dead flesh falling off, "can I even go outside in the sun? Will the light destroy me?"

"That only happens to vampires," my secretary (who was naked) said.

"Then I'll be okay?" I asked her.

"I don't see why not," she said.

"I'll have to use your car."

"The keys are on the kitchen table," she said. "Before you go, will you give me a sloppy kiss?"

"But of course," and I gave her a long one.

The sunlight didn't put an end to my being one of the undead, but I can't say it was all that pleasant. The heat and brightness were extremely annoying; and it was a sunny day with no clouds to boot. I couldn't believe that it was this very sun that made me move to southern Florida in the first place.

I drove to South Beach and turned on the radio. The local news was reporting on "riots and madness" on the streets of Miami.

"It is uncertain if this could be college students protesting the war," the news announcer said, "or some other form of civil unrest and disobedience."

"Hippies," I muttered, "goddamn hippies."

I heard a lot of police and ambulance sirens, but didn't see any signs of rioting or madness.

The apartment complex where the orgy had taken place four nights ago was covered in yellow police tape.

There was one lone cop guarding it. He was young and in uniform and looked nervous. When he saw me, he drew his service revolver, pointed it at me and said, "Stop right there you freak!"

"Freak?" I said incredulously, and then I remembered what I looked like.

"It's okay," I said. "Really."

"The hell it is. You just turn around and go back to what rock you crawled out from."

"Or what?"

"Or I'll shoot."

"Why don't you shoot, rookie," I told him, "because I don't think it'll do a goddamn thing to me."

Seemed like good a time as any to test this. The rookie shot me once, in the chest. I felt the impact but there was no pain. There was a hole, but there was no blood.

"Holy crap," said the rookie.

All I could do was laugh, and the laughter brought out the apparent monster inside of me. I moved fast, slapping the gun out of the rookie's hand. "No, please," he said and this made me laugh more — like a maniac — and just as it overtook me last night, there was the sudden urge and need; so I bashed the rookie's head on the ground, opening his skull, and feasted on his squishy, yummy brains, savoring each bite. I could feel the brain matter and various fluids going down my throat and settling into my stomach. This felt good. But do the dead eat? I couldn't be completely dead then. Those people at the orgy, I saw them all die, rather violently, their brains being devoured by The Power and his buddies.

What the fuck. I got a hold of myself. With my jacket sleeve, I wiped mind goo away from my mouth.

I stepped under the police tape and into the apartment. Empty, as expected, with the walls and floors covered in dried, putrid blood. Lots of chalked outlines of bodies, many bodies.

... and then a voice.

Arthur Gideon.
"What?"
Gideon, why didn't you do as I told you?
"Tell me what? Where are you?"
Why didn't you do as I told you?
It was The Power. His voice was in my head.
"Get out of my skull, you motherfucker."
You are one of us now.
Distant laughter.
Go home, Arthur Gideon.
"Fuck you."
Go home, we're waiting.

***

On the radio, the news guy was saying, " ... strange and unconfirmed reports that dozens of bodies are missing from the police morgue. These bodies are from a mass murder that happened several nights ago ..."

Ah, but it was true. Now I knew what was going on because I saw them all over town: naked and ugly zombies wandering around with that special zombie walk and causing all kinds of dastardly trouble, like killing hapless ordinary citizens on the streets.

***

The Power held Miss Melfile with one arm and had a gun to her head, the same pistol he used on me. His buddies were there, too, as well as Jenna Rush. Jenna was not the tanned pretty hippie girl anymore; she was like me, like The Power, like all her friends who were now terrorizing Miami.

"Gideon! We *just* missed each other," said The Power. "We got here and you'd *just* taken off. And *look* what you left for us, one hot bitch." He kissed Ms. Melfile on the cheek; she was struggling but didn't seem to mind. I don't think The Power realized she was into dead men.

Still, I said, for effect: "Let her go."

"That's what you blabbered last time."

"And now *look at me*," Jenna Rush said with a giggle.

"Before you were killed," said The Power, "I told you when you came back, you were to go to see the Senator and tell him about his daughter. You didn't do this. Tsk tsk tsk."

"Yeah," said one of his crew, "tsk."

The others went, "Tsk tsk tsk."

"Don't you know I'm the leader of you all?" said The Power. "I'm the fucken wellspring, pal!"

"We all do what he says," Jenna Rush giggled.

"The problem here," I said, "is that I've always had a problem with authority."

"You'd make a great hippie, Gideon. I had a feeling you'd be difficult. This is a-okay. So: here we are. And this is what I want you to do, Mr. Private Eyeball: you're going to call the Senator, you're going to say you have his little girl, and you're going to set up a meet with him. Say she's being stubborn, she doesn't want to go home, so you want them to have a father-daughter heart-to-heart on neutral ground. The meeting place will be where we killed and buried you. Nice and remote."

"And if I don't?"

"Your hot bitch here gets a bullet in the noggin."

"Let him shoot me, Arty," Ms. Melfile said. "Don't give in to ultimatums from assholes."

"Ahh, honey, you don't mean that," said The Power, kissing her cheek again.

"Arty," my secretary said, looking right at me, "you must realize now what I truly want."

"Yes," I said.

"Just let him do it."

"I can't. This has to play out to an end."

She nodded.

"Do I kill her or not?" The Power asked.

I wanted to get to the bottom of this shit. I went to the phone and called the Senator's private line.

"Goddammit," he said, "I've been trying to reach you the past 48 hours!"

"I have her."

"You found her?"

"She's here."

"Good job, sir. And not a moment too soon; this city is going to hell right now."

"Literally."

"Bring her home."

"She won't go."

"What?"

I held the phone toward Jenna.

She yelled, "FUCK YOU DADDY I WON'T GO HOME!"

I proposed the meet.

"I'll be there in thirty minutes," he said.

"Half an hour," I said to The Power, hanging up the phone.

"Works for me," he said with a shrug.

"Now let my secretary go."

"I'm a zombie of my word," he said, and released Ms. Melfile from his grip.

She straightened her hair and smoothed down her skirt. She didn't look at me. Ms. Melfile appeared disappointed.

***

That remote area just outside the city limits didn't seem so desolate and lonely in the daytime. Senator Rush showed up in his car with Jill and two bodyguards donning dark suits — I had no idea if they were federal or private; they were your typical thugs: well-dressed and armed and willing to kill on command. Jenna Rush and I stood by Ms. Melfile's car and waited. (I still had no idea where my car was, probably stolen or vandalized.) Jenna kept giggling, saying, "Man oh man is Daddy having the surprise of his lifetime coming."

"Quiet," I said. "You like being this way?"

"What about you? We're the same, we're part of The Power now. He's going to rule the world in a month."

"Don't get caught up in that fellow's delusions of grandeur," I said.

"You know it's true. You can feel it. *I know you can feel it.* All us zombies, we're connected, man."

"Hush. Your father is here."

"You just don't know," Jenna said, "it's Daddy's fault we're like this now!"

"Jenna!" the Senator cried out. He stopped when he got a good look at his daughter and me: walking corpses on a sunny day and not smelling anything like a bed of roses. "Sweet baby Jesus," he said, stumbling. Jill and one of his bodyguards caught him. "Dear Lord," he moaned, "you've been turned into one of those monsters."

"And you're the monster maker, Senator," said The Power.

I have no idea where his voice came from; it boomed like there were hidden loudspeakers. The Power and his men emerged from the ground, where they had buried themselves. They moved fast, overtaking Rush's two men before they could react, breaking their arms and legs and necks with an admirable swiftness.

Then they took care of Jill. She screamed, she tried to fight them. She died in a great deal of pain, and The Power's men took delight in her agony and blood. I have to admit I felt a tinge of glee myself, after the snotty way the woman had treated me during our last encounter. Then I recalled what Rush had told me: find his daughter, I could have Jill in bed. I wondered if Jill was like Ms. Melfile and preferred dead men over live flesh.

There were four of us standing in a face-off: Jenna and her father, The Power and yours truly.

"What on earth are you?" asked the Senator as The Power took a step in his direction. "You're one of those things from the flying saucers, aren't you? I read the Roswell report."

"Don't you recognize me, Mr. Rush?" said The Power. "I used to be human, until you and your rich compadres sent me and my buddies to Vietnam."

"Excuse me?"

"Don't lie, Daddy," Jenna said.

"What have you done to my daughter, you sick bastard?!?"

"Exactly what you did to me," said The Power.

"What you did to all of us," said The Power's crew, in unison.

"Listen, whatever in blazes you are," Rush said, "I have no idea what you're talking about."

"My name is Lieutenant Steven Carl Fitzsimmons," said The Power. He took a soldier's stance of attention and saluted. "*Sir!*" The other five also saluted and yelled, "Sir, yes, sir!"

The Senator's jaw dropped and his face turned ... gray.

"Ahhhh," said The Power, "recognition."

"This isn't possible. You and your platoon ... are dead."

"Yes, *yes* we are. And we happen to be here for some payback. You see, Mr. Gideon," and The Power turned his rotting skull my way, "Senator Rush is on what you would call a Black Project Committee, a little unknown wing of the Intelligence Arm of the Senate. And our people's representative here championed a nifty little project to create an unstoppable, unkillable Marine. Well, the Marine could die in combat, but he'd come back. Usually takes two or three days for the stuff they injected into us to take effect. And what did they put in our blood? Activated only when the heart stops beating? Something cooked up in a secret buried lab? No. An ancient recipe he got from a voodoo priestess from Haiti. She gives him the recipe, she and her family get to come to Florida and prosper as bonafide United States citizens. Was that the deal, Senator?"

"You keep your mouth *shut,*" said Rush. "You're discussing top secret information. You signed an oath of —"

"Yeah? And what will you do to me? Have me executed for treason?"

The Power and his men laughed.

Jenna Rush laughed.

I started to laugh.

The Power continued: "Well, my platoon was selected as lab rats. They injected us, told us it was in case we got bit by bad insects in the jungle. Fucking liars, but what do you expect from the government? To cut to the nitty-gritty, Senator, the recipe worked. Me and my men were killed in an ambush. A few days later we rose from the dead and we hunted down those gooks who killed us and them a bunch of zombies too."

"You went MIA," said Rush.

"We came home, for payback."

"You need to report back to your unit, your base. Immediately, Lieutenant! I can have you tossed in Leavenworth for this!"

The zombies laughed more.

"When I heard your daughter was a runaway," said The Power, "well, I came up with a *grand* idea for revenge."

"It's horrible what you did to these cool guys, Daddy," Jenna said. "But in the end, it all works out. I like being a zombie. It's the most far out thing ever."

"Oh my God," said Rush. "Oh no ... "

"And now you're going to join us," said The Power.

"No."

"Yes."

"No."

"*Yes.*"

The Power's men held the Senator down.

"My sweet dear little one," The Power said to Jenna, "would you do the honors?"

"I'd love to." Jenna picked up a large rock and approached her father. "It'll hurt, Daddy, but in a couple of days everything will be all right and you'll thank me."

The Senator screamed and his daughter cracked opened his head and began to eat.

I turned and started to get into Ms. Melfile's car.

The Power joined me, sitting in the passenger's seat.

"Ahhh, brains," he said. "It's like candy to a girl. What do brains taste like to you, private eye guy?"

"Steak."

"Pork to me. I'm a bacon man."

"Can I drive you anywhere?"

"Nah. So you're not pissed off?"

"What can I do now?"

"It's all his fault," and he gestured to the body of Rush.

"Warmongers," I said.

"You understand what's happening," said The Power.

"All of Miami will be zombies within the week."

"And the state, and the country, and the world."

"With you as leader?"

He shrugged. "Who knows."

"I'm not a follower."

"I see that now. Join me anyway."

"I have my own life to live," I said, "as a zombie."

"Well," he said, "you know where to find me."

VII
"Zombie lovers"

There were zombies everywhere in the city and it wasn't so bad; I was one of them and getting used to their presence.

I drove home. Lissa Melfile wasn't there.

I picked up the phone but the phone line was dead (no pun intended here).

I drove to my office.

My secretary was there, and she was naked.

"This is a sight," I said.

"I wanted you to see me like this," she said.

"I like what I see."

"I don't. Arty, I don't. You know what I want, what I need. Right?"

I nodded. "I've been thinking about it."

"It's some sort of form of evolution," she said. "And I've been waiting for this all my life."

***

Two and a half days later, she woke up in bed. Her flesh was no longer white and pink. Her brains, I must admit, were delicious, the best I've ever had.

"Oh, Arty!" she said, holding out her arms.

I went to her and we made love the way zombies do it, and let me tell you: it's the best I've ever had.

Later, I asked her, "What happens when the whole world becomes a race a zombies? What do we do then?"

"We grow," she said, and she was right.

ALL THE PRETTY GIRLS
by Ronald Damien Malfi

What do you know?

He knew where he was, for one thing. The day was hot and without wind, the jagged sandstone bluffs cresting like whitecaps above the darkened line of ponderosa pines. Sniffing the still air, Pablo Santiago could smell trout from the river, metallic and fishy, like ointment. Before him, Chama River Canyon lay undisturbed and contemplating, as if deep in thought. The hot sun beating down on his shoulders, Santiago fondly recalled the days of his youth fishing along the cusp of the winding river. On many occasions he'd trekked through the pinon-juniper woodlands, ensconced in the scenic hug of Apache plume and cliffrose and fendlerbush, only to arrive exhausted but content at the El Vado Lake Dam. In his youth, he'd spent many evenings watching the sun deteriorate beyond the horizon, bruising the sky with a multitude of pastel hues while sipping dandelion wine and smoking Pall Malls.

What do you know?

He knew about the car, too. And in many ways, despite all his years living off the land — despite the countless elk and coyotes he'd trapped and killed and eaten; despite his unwavering respect for the land itself — he knew the car was most important. How he'd come across it no longer mattered (anyway, he couldn't remember) and how it had gotten there, wedged between the blue-tinted firs along the cusp of the valley like a forgotten relic, was not important. What was important — what genuinely *mattered* — was what the car really *was*.

What do you know?

A lot, Pablo Santiago thought. Over time, he'd come to know a lot.

On the outside, it was a 1962 Mercury Comet S-22 Coupe with a two-tone black and red paint job, rusted and scored and pocked by the elements. Its windshield was grimy and covered in bull's-eye cracks. Its tires were flattened and flaking with rot and, over time, had become part of the earth. Its Mylar door panels were pitted and ruined, the bucket seats and loop carpeting torn and cancerous with mold. The front grille, with its busted-out quad-headlamps and deluxe chrome, was a mouth crowded with teeth, rusty and sharp for biting.

This day, in the hot sunshine, Santiago crossed down into the valley, the rising, rocky tumult of Albiquiu behind him, and paused beneath a tall stand of firs. They provided much shade in the summer, and he stood there for several moments while he mopped his brow with an oily hand towel. He thought of the trout in the river and the smell of them in the air. From where he stood he could not see the car, but some animal part of him could sense it. Santiago was not a stupid man, nor was he irreligious: he knew divinity when confronted with it. It was a power, he knew, which was even greater than the power of the land.

Leaving the stand of firs, Santiago advanced toward the lip of the canyon. From here, he could hear the din of the river and could smell brine in the air. Knowing the water was so close was enough to cool and refresh his body, and he found his legs suddenly pumping stronger and harder than they had just moments ago. Earlier in the summer, it had been a difficult hike with the equipment — the shovel, the spade, the rake, the pickaxe — but he'd soon gotten accustomed to his work and began stowing his tools in the Comet's back seat. The fresh earth smell left behind by the tools smelled better than the car's interior anyway, and it was easier for Santiago to breathe when seated behind the Comet's steering wheel. Smelled better than the stink from the trunk ...

Ahead, a clearing opened up and Santiago could see the Comet's grinning grillwork behind a thin veil of kudzu. Shade from the surrounding firs made it look dull and dusty. Hitching up his dungarees, Santiago approached the vehicle, his eyes tracing the lines of the exterior, running over the chassis, hunting for a glimpse of reflected sunlight in the chrome. But there was none this day; there was too much shade beneath the trees.

If I could get you to run, Santiago thought, *we would not be so limited to Chama Canyon.* He thought, *We would not be limited to the grasslands up north and the Rio Grande and Albiquiu. If I could get you to run,* he thought, *we could travel and not be limited to any single place.*

But there was no way. Pablo Santiago was not a mechanic and knew nothing about getting old cars to run. The 6-cylinder engine beneath the Comet's hood could have been a birdcage or a ball of yarn or a series of intertwined coat-hangers. Often, Santiago found himself staring at the dead engine, one bronze and meaty hand propping up the hood, examining the intricacies of the object like a mathematician scrutinizing an equation. The engine, he knew, was the heart. If only he could get the heart beating again …

He shook his head and took a step away from the vehicle. He'd been staring at his mottled reflection in the grimy driver's side window. Beads of perspiration had broken out across his upper lip. He removed his hand towel from the rear pocket of his dungarees and blotted his face. The towel reeked of motor oil, dirt and something like copper. He quickly stuffed it back in his trousers.

Sometimes the car bled motor oil. In a black trail, it would slide down through the rocks toward the edge of the cliff. If he didn't blot it up in time, it would spill into the river below. And that wouldn't be good. Santiago did not know why he thought this, but he knew it just the same as he knew his own name. Something about that oil spilling into the river would be *muy mal.*

If I could get you to run, he thought now, *I wouldn't have to worry about this river.*

He stepped around to the rear of the car, one hand fisted around a tree branch for support, and examined the ground. There was no oil. He felt a wave of relief wash over him. Peering over the cliff, he could see the extended branches of shrubbery down the cliff-face, and could see the stacked layers of colored rock, stacked like textbooks, dipping down toward the river and the canyon floor. The river looked black and like gasoline in the sun.

What do you know?

He knew what to do. And he would waste no more time.

Santiago carried a slender metal prong on a key ring. He removed this device from the pocket of his pants now, examined it briefly in the hot sun, and moved toward the Comet's trunk. Here he paused, as if waiting for a signal. Listened. In his head, he counted: seven days. Always seven. He ran his eyes over the trunk. His reflection stared back at him from the black paint, dusty and pierced with tiny dents. Santiago ran two fingers over the trunk. Even in the shade of the firs, the steel was hot, warmed by the midday sun.

He slid the metal prong into the trunk's keyhole and maneuvered the prong around until he felt the lock give. There was a hollow metallic clang. Absentmindedly, he remained with one hand on top of the trunk, holding it down against the force of the springs. The trunk wanted to open, but the springs were weak with age and Santiago held the trunk down without difficulty.

There will be many black bears here before the summer is out, he thought without interest, his eyes focused on the wealth of trees and shrubbery through which he had come. *There will be plenty before the days get shorter and the nights get colder. I can remember all this land before it was government land, and how my father and grandfather had shot many black bears along this ridge. The bears,* he thought, *they are smart, smarter than we think, and if you shoot them and don't kill them, they will run for the cliff and run off and fall into the river and die. They will die either way but they do not want to die and bring satisfaction to the one bringing its death. They are noble that way.*

He thought he felt something thump against the bottom of the trunk and that made his heart skip in his thick chest. But no — it was all in his head, and he uttered a skittish, almost girlish laugh. Then opened the trunk.

At this point, something always overtook Pablo Santiago, and that was good. Not a spirit or any such thing but, rather, a certain *drive,* enabling him to function almost without senses: practically blind and deaf and without touch or smell. Like a long-distance runner. He operated like a machine, if only for the time it took to remove the carcass from the Comet's trunk and dump it to the earth, but that was time enough. That was the hardest part. The hardest part was always opening the trunk and seeing those dead eyes staring up from the black maw of the trunk ... the gray cheesecloth look of the skin ... the lips, always pulled back in a frozen snarl, the gums purple ... fingernails shorn away ...

Eyes slightly unfocused, Santiago exhaled heavily while wiping his forehead with the heel of one hand. He wasn't aggravated, not even disappointed anymore. Some part of him felt the tingling sensation of failure, but it was so minute that he hardly acknowledged it. Now was not a time to contemplate failure. Now was a time to be done with it and move on.

Santiago bent over the lip of the trunk and stuffed his large hands beneath the armpits of the body. The carcass was of a nude young woman, seven days dead, and soggy and heavy on the bottom where her remaining bodily fluids had come to settle. Such was the way with dehydration. Brittle skin, sunken eyes, soggy underside. The reek of urine and feces so strong from the trunk, it made Santiago's eyes water, and he worked quickly to hoist the body from the trunk and let it spill to the rocky earth. The body was not heavy, but even the solitary act of lifting seemed to wear him out. He removed a small bladder bag from his belt loop, popped the cap, and delicately sipped some water. It felt good and cold and clean. He poured some into his cupped left hand, then proceeded to dampen his brow and the sweaty nape of his neck. Some water ran down his shirt collar, chilling him.

Displeased with the smell of the trunk, Santiago quickly slammed it shut. The sound seemed to echo out over the canyon and across the valley like a gunshot. Looking down at the pallid, emaciated ruin at his feet, still vaguely female even in such a state, he was again prodded by that dull, throbbing sense of failure.

Is it me? he couldn't help but wonder. It was not the first time. *Do none of them take because of me?*

Her breasts had flattened to her chest, the nipples like two graying dimples of flesh. The abrupt mound of her pubis, sparsely peppered with fine black hairs, reminded him of the kudzu and the underbrush that made up the floor of Chama River Canyon. Her legs clamped together in a fetal stiffness, his eyes running over the twisted and bony knobs of her knees, Santiago was suddenly and frighteningly overcome by the urge to *separate* those legs, force them apart, and resume the act once again — one last time — if only to regain some sort of personal composure, some sense of self-gratification and accomplishment. Had he failed *again?* And how long until he proved useless and the car —

No. He wouldn't think about that. Anyway, there was work to do.

Retrieving his tools from the Comet's back seat, Pablo Santiago carried them to a remote tract of land further down the canyon ridge. Here, the ground was mostly rock and sand, difficult and tedious for digging, but devoid of any foliage that might appear suspicious if uprooted. He knew this land well, had grown up knowing it, and recognized each individual sandstone flat like a man recognizes old friends in a photograph. He knew the slope of the valley, the stonier parts of the earth. He also knew where the other bodies were buried, all those pretty girls, and was careful to weave around these sacred places when walking to a fresh spot.

He selected an undisturbed spot of land and dug a shallow grave. The sun was hot on his back while he worked and his mind was occupied with the sound of the rushing river in the canyon below. A portage straight to the heart of the Rio Grande, Pablo Santiago was quietly enraptured by the unmitigated freedom of the river, immune from obligation and unconstrained by a lack of duty. Unlike the sedentary Comet, the river could be anywhere in the world given enough time. *Anywhere.* The notion fascinated Santiago, and several times he paused during his dig to lean on the carved wooden handle of his shovel and contemplate the enormity of such a thing.

It was getting on dusk when he returned to the Comet for the woman's body. Propping it over one immense shoulder, Santiago carried the corpse easily to the fresh hole in the earth. He could feel the presence of the car boring into his back as he laid the woman's body into the hole. While he filled the hole with dirt he was aware of the wind whistling and sighing through the rust-holes along the vehicle's chassis.

We are getting close now, he promised the Comet. *I can feel how close we are getting. It is only a matter of time. We must be patient. It will work out.*

He filled in the grave and raked over the disturbed soil. Then, with the tools slung over his shoulder, he hiked back to the car.

The driver's side door stood open. He did not remember leaving it open, but that didn't matter. With the Comet, such things were not unusual. Carefully, he replaced his tools in the Comet's back seat, then — after a long pause — slid into the driver's seat and pulled the door shut.

He sat in silence, staring at the filth covered windshield. He had been doing this for many months now, and still he was not quite used to it. Had he discovered the car one afternoon while driving his truck down the main highway? No; it was impossible to see the car from the highway, particularly in the summer when the forestry was in bloom. Had he spotted it one evening while fishing near El Vado Lake Dam? No; the car was hidden from sight at such a distance. One would require the eyes of a hawk. So he could not remember how he had found the car, but he could guess that he was probably drawn to it somehow, beckoned, summoned, called to it. Somehow. And he had come.

He sat behind the Comet's steering wheel for a long time. The interior smelled like urine and blood and dirt and mildew. At times, in the stillness of the car, his mind dredged up the sounds of all the pretty girls he'd struggled with in the back seat. He'd lost count of the bodies, each one a failure, each one unworthy. Or was *he* unworthy? Was his *seed* unworthy?

No, he told himself. *I was chosen. How could I be unworthy if I was chosen?*

But perhaps the car made a mistake ...

"God does not make mistakes," he said aloud. His voice

sounded thick and deep in the confines of the car and he did not like it.

Through the filthy windshield he watched the sun set behind the dark brown crags. His eyelids felt lazy and he wanted to sleep. But work was not done. There would be no sleep until work —

A low, electrical hum filled the car. Santiago could both feel and hear it. He gripped the four-spoked steering wheel with two hands and squeezed tight. He could feel the current — faint but undeniably there — tracing up his arms. The dash lights flickered, flickered, glowed, and the radio dial bled an eerie green light onto Santiago's lap. Static hissed from the radio. Santiago watched as the dial spun on its own, the vertical red pin sliding left and right and left again as if attempting to locate a signal. The static grew louder, rattling the ancient speakers. Santiago could feel the current in his teeth now, his back teeth and the bones of his skull.

"Are you angry, Lord?" Santiago half-whispered, his eyes locked on the illuminated radio dial. "Do not be angry." The car's shaking caused his voice to vibrate. "She was not the right one. I will find the right one. I need more time."

The *shhh-shhh* of static.

"How many?" Santiago asked.

Shhh-shhh.

"That many? Already?" Had he really gone through six women in all this time? He'd lost count, but he hadn't thought the number was so high. It bothered him to think he'd failed so frequently.

"There will be more," he promised the car. "It is summer. There are always more."

The static grew louder.

"Tonight?" Santiago said. "I think ..."

The dashboard lights flickered and the radio dial spun wildly.

"All right," promised Pablo Santiago, "I will find one tonight." Then, as an afterthought: "But it is getting *muy* risky. Soon, there will be many people asking many questions. Too many girls, the police will surely start looking at me. It is only a matter of time."

The car shuddered, the dashboard lights flickered. The radio grew louder and louder until it crested, then died completely. The flickering lights went out. The car was once again silent and still.

Pablo Santiago's god was a 1962 Mercury Comet.

It was dark when Santiago returned to the Monastery of Christ abbey deep in the canyon. He pulled his pickup truck down a rocky path, got out, and headed directly to the *case del rio* where he was employed as groundskeeper for the retreat's guesthouses. In his small one-room shack, Santiago washed his face and drank a tall glass of water. The water was good and cold. There was some frozen river trout in an ice chest. He considered broiling some fish but decided he was not hungry. Instead, he pulled on a weather-worn anorak, crept out of the shack, and used a set of keys to gain entrance to the main lobby of the guesthouse. Here, he moved quietly down the hall and slipped through an access door that communicated with a large, darkened room. It was here that the inner-workings of the guesthouse had been in operation before the monastery changed over to solar power.

There were some tools here, and some items in unlabeled mason jars on shelves. Pablo Santiago went directly to a crowbar hanging from a pegboard, pulled it down, and carried it back into the guesthouse lobby.

There were many rooms here. From behind a number of doors he could hear the shrill din of laughter, unintentionally disrespectful to the cenobitic life of the Benedictine monks. These were tourists, were visitors, were people who paid their money to stay at the monastery and go fishing and hiking and canoeing. *Los intrusos*, many of the locals called them. There were many small villages throughout Chama River Canyon comprised of several generations of Hispanic immigrants. These were people who had worked the land and had lived off it since their forefathers crossed the Mexico border. There were many girls there, ripe enough for Santiago and his God, but none of his victims ever came from these villages, and not out of any sense of heritage or pride or respect but — simply —

out of concern that he would be caught too quickly. It was easier to forget about strangers when they disappeared.

Using another key, Santiago gained access to one of these rooms. They were small rooms, with a bed and a single window beside the bed, an adjoining bathroom, a closet for hanging clothing, a dresser opposite the bed, and a mirror on the wall above the dresser. Also, a hand-carved wooden cross on the wall. Modest yet expensive rooms.

There was a suitcase on the bed but no one in the room. Still carrying the crowbar, Santiago slid open the closet door and stepped inside. Behind him, he pulled the door closed but not all the way, allowing a vertical sliver of space through which he could keep an eye on the room.

They are out looking for mountain lion, Pablo Santiago thought as he sat Indian-style on the carpeted floor of the closet. *And why not? They come here from big cities and pay good money to see them. It is not as if they see mountain lion every day.*

Pulling up the hood of the anorak, Pablo Santiago waited. He had patience much like the mountain lion.

What do you know?

Sound. And opening his eyes he was aware he'd fallen asleep. Or almost. But it did not take him any time to recall his surroundings: on the closet floor in one of the guestrooms. The noise that had woken him: the sound of the guestroom door opening. Also, the gay sound of drunken laughter.

These tourists, Santiago thought, peeking through the space in the closet door, *all they know to do is drink. Litter and spend their money and drink-drink-drink.* Los borrachos!

Two figures moved past the closet. Lights were turned on. More laughter. A man and a woman. He tried to see the woman but he could not see her face. She moved too quickly. The man, though — he was young and handsome and, Santiago thought, very white. As he sat crouched in their closet, he could hear bits and pieces of their conversation ...

"I've never seen so much food," the very white man said. "And all the wine! Have you ever seen such wine?"

"I didn't think it would be this way at all," said the woman.

Santiago still could not see her. "I didn't want to come but now I'm glad we're here."

Sí, Santiago thought, *as am I.*

"It is beautiful here," the woman continued. She moved across the room and went to the suitcase on the bed. Santiago could see her back. She was tall and slender with a petite waist and long, dark hair. Wringing the crowbar between his hands, he could feel the crotch of his dungarees tightening.

"Beautiful," the man agreed, "but very dusty. It's on all my clothes."

"You complain," said the woman.

"I'm sorry."

"It's nothing. It's perfect. Go and shower and then I'll shower."

"Yes, you're right," the man said. "It *is* perfect." And disappeared into the bathroom, closing the door behind him.

From where he sat, perched and anxious as if on a ledge, Pablo Santiago watched the woman cross the room and advance toward the mirror above the dresser. In her maneuvering, he caught a glimpse of her reflection in the glass. She was very beautiful.

Weren't they all? he thought, watching her. *Weren't they all pretty girls?*

The woman began fixing her hair in the mirror. The sound of running water could be heard from the bathroom. Then the man's low, baritone singing. This made the woman smile at her reflection. She removed her blouse and unhooked her bra, tossing the articles onto the bed. Her breasts were small and neat and pink. Santiago watched as she moved again to the suitcase, rummaged around for something, then went over to the single window beside the bed and pushed it open a few inches. Santiago heard the click of a lighter and saw a spark. The woman lit what appeared to be a joint, raped it of three quick sucks, then exhaled through the open window.

Breathing heavy, Santiago managed to stand in the cramped closet space. Holding the crowbar in one hand, the seat of his dungarees pulling tighter and tighter, he slid open the closet door. It made no sound; groundskeeper Santiago was meticulous about oiling all hinges and tracks. He moved across the carpet slowly, familiar enough to avoid every groaning floorboard, listening to the soundtrack of the very white man singing in the shower. A few paces behind the woman, his shadow not yet on the wall beside her own (he was very conscious of this), Santiago felt that same sense of *drive* overtake him, quite similar to the feeling that rushed through his body when he had to pull his failures from the Comet's trunk ... and very nearly the same as how he felt when overtaking them in the Comet's back seat ...

But no — he was thinking too much ahead of himself and that was bad. To think ahead was to pay little attention to the present. And after six failures, as the Comet had reminded him, he could afford no more —

The woman sensed him, turned and stared. It seemed like an eternity, as it always did, and Pablo Santiago was able to examine the split ends of her hair, the broken blood vessels in her sclera, the knobs of gooseflesh that had broken out along her body, and the erect state of her nipples. And he sensed a scream rising up her throat — but not of fear, merely of surprise, of utter ridiculous and absurd surprise — and he raised the crowbar and brought it down across the upper right side of her head. It stunned her, rocked her head back on her neck, but did not knock her out. It *did* kill the scream, killing it even before it came, like an abortion. One hand went back and slapped a palm against the wall while her other hand dropped the joint on the bedspread. Before striking the woman again, Santiago carefully picked the joint off the bedspread and pinched the cherry dead, as to not start a fire. Too many fires had devastated the land over the years, and they all began very small and very harmless.

"What do you know, *mi* paramour?" Santiago whispered, and struck the woman a second time. This time, she went down.

Santiago wasted no time gathering the woman's supine body from the bedspread and arranging her over one shoulder as if she were a small Christmas tree and he a lumberjack. Still listening to the singing man in the shower, Santiago crossed the room, opened the door, and looked up and down the hallway. It was empty, but he need not walk the length of it; rather, he darted into a second doorway that connected with a long corridor used only in case of fires. The woman was very light on his shoulder as he hurried along and he thought that she was perfect, that she would be the one, and there would be no failure this time. God would be pleased.

At the end of the hallway, Santiago pushed through the exit and out into the freezing night. It is a misconception that nighttime in the desert is mild and pleasant. If Pablo Santiago had a quarter for every story he heard about someone freezing to death in the desert, he would be a very rich man.

Crossing the rocky tarmac with the woman over his shoulder, her skin now cold to the touch in the frigid night air, Santiago hurried around a copse of pines and headed without pause to his pickup parked outside his tiny shack. There, he quickly wrapped the woman's body in a piece of tarpaulin, tied it, and eased her down in the bed of the truck. Crawling behind the steering wheel, he then turned over the engine, pulled the transmission into reverse, and rolled slowly backward down the gravel drive. Only once he was back on the main highway that overlooked the canyon did he begin to relax. It could have taken him an hour or fifteen minutes to wrap the woman in the tarp — he could not remember. And was she number six or seven? Or was he just getting confused with the seven days he had to wait before opening the trunk again? Damn it, his mind was going on him. Old age creeping, the dirty devil.

The drive to the canyon ridge where the car sat waiting was lonely. Above, the moon was full and pearl-colored. The road below was bumpy and could prove treacherous at night. Many times Santiago had not seen a jagged rock or mule deer carcass in the dark and had blown a flat. Now, he rationalized, would be a poor time for flats.

Once he reached the clearing, Santiago drove the pickup right up to the ridge of the canyon. Outside, the sky was dense with stars. Santiago went directly to the truck bed and quickly unraveled the tarpaulin from the woman's body. As the cold night air struck the woman's bare chest, she began to stir and moan and flutter her eyes. She was bleeding badly from the gash at the side of her head. Santiago hoisted her from the bed and carried her in his arms to the silent and brooding Mercury Comet. It looked smarter in the dark, the car, as if it had set aside all pretenses and fakery used to manipulate Santiago in the daylight. Now, in the dark, there was no need for such formalities. In the dark, things were what they were.

The woman began forming words just as Santiago slid her into the Comet's back seat. Hunching into the car himself, he planted one foot down on the business end of the shovel and the handle shot up and thudded against the roof of the car, startling him. Then he laughed nervously and pulled the tools from the car and set them against a tree. *Muy estupido.* It wasn't the first time that had happened.

Strewn out along the back seats, the woman brought a hand up to her face, her head. She was still moaning but was making no sense. Santiago knew he would have to be quick if it was to be easiest, and he leaned forward and proceeded to unbuckle her slacks. He tugged them off her hips, along with her underwear, and bent to remove her shoes — and saw that one of her shoes was missing. Surely she had been wearing both shoes when he carried her from the retreat, yes?

Not now, he thought. *Now is time for action, not thought. There will be plenty of time to think about things later.*

Yanking the remaining clothes from her body, Pablo Santiago remained poised and motionless above the woman, breathing deeply, his eyes creeping along her flesh. There was a sweetness to this act still, and that at least made it bearable, but there was also that goddamn *drive,* too, and that was now burning up inside him. Again, he could feel himself swelling inside his dungarees. The woman — her body was gorgeous and white and smooth and pink and perfect and firm and he could see the tiny faded scars along her blue-tinted flesh and the smattering of freckles and the fine white hairs covering her breasts and her belly, and the soft downy mat of dark hair between her thighs, and the gradual incline and *receive* of her legs and the way they bent and straightened and looked blue and white and perfect in the moonlight filtering through the dirty rear windshield.

Breathing heavy, struggling now with his own pants, Pablo Santiago said, "You may consider a retreat for your personal gratification. We are not beyond compassion. God is love." He had spoken these words many times before. "I recommend summoning the image of the great and mighty mule deer, dark and stunning and graceful and mysterious in nature." He'd had time to rehearse these words. "The mule deer is a powerful animal and is capable of many great things, *pero* the mule deer is also a gentle and serene animal who favors nature and peace."

His zipper undone, Pablo Santiago separated his victim's legs and forced himself between them. Beneath him, he felt the woman's body go stiff and knew she was about to start screaming, but that didn't matter out here. No one would hear her, not for miles. Just him. And God.

He continued, "The mule deer of this habitat run with a series of distinct leaps and bounds. This is called 'stotting,' and," he went on, his breathing labored now, his actions muddying his thoughts, "and ... and this is significant because it is typical only of mule deer from ... *from* ... "

The car began to hum beneath him and just as he felt his seed lurch from him, completing the act, the car's radio came instantly to life, hissing and spitting with static. Eyes pressed closed, Santiago could hear nothing but that hissing *shhh-shhh* of static and the shrieks from the struggling woman pinned beneath his great weight. And he could feel nothing but the hum of the vehicle all around him and the wasted, shriveled sensation of release.

The woman screamed.

"What do you know?" Pablo Santiago shouted back. "Just tell me what you know!"

He dragged her from the car. She was kicking and struggling and moaning now, but her struggles were without power. The two blows she'd received from the crowbar had knocked something loose in her head, Santiago assumed. That, too, had happened before.

With little difficulty he carried her to the rear of the vehicle. The cold night air now felt good against Santiago's skin, freezing the sweat on his body. The Comet's trunk stood open. Santiago had not opened it. Sometimes this happened and sometimes it did not. It didn't matter now, anyway.

Santiago lifted the slumped and struggling woman up over the lip of the Comet's trunk and let her fall into the gaping black maw. Again he was accosted with the ripe, fetid smell of the trunk's interior. *Maybe not all of them have died from heat or cold or starvation,* Santiago thought now. *Maybe at least one died from that smell.*

But there would be no dying this time. This time, there would be no failure. He would see. After seven days, he would see.

Pablo Santiago slammed the trunk closed with the nude woman inside and remained with both his palms planted to the top of the trunk, motionless, for some time. Closing his eyes, he could still feel the vehicle humming beneath his palms, electrical currents juicing up his arms. He did not like to feel this, did not like to think of this. Instead, he thought of the river trout and the way they often swallowed lures and hooks and, most often, all the bait. There were nice size trout in the river, Santiago knew. He'd fished it for many years and the river had been kind to him and he, in turn, had remained true to the river.

He righted himself, gathering his tools, and piled them in the back seat of the Comet. Then, sitting behind the steering wheel, he said, "This time, my Lord, will be the time. I make these promises," he explained to the car, "because I know this to be true in *el corazón.*"

The car did not respond. All Santiago could hear was the muffled sobs and relentless pounding coming from the Comet's trunk. Such sounds hurt his ears. How at ease he would feel once his God was finally sated.

This time, he promised himself now, *this time. No more because it will be this time.*

He knew what to expect upon returning to the abbey. There were two police cruisers outside, their lights flashing, and many *policía* inside the monastery. This did little to disturb the composure of Pablo Santiago, and only when a policeman spoke his name did he look up at all.

"Pablo Santiago?" The policeman was young and hungry-looking, in the way most black bears get when they are late in hibernating and cannot find food. "Sir?"

"Yes," Santiago said, pausing just outside the circle of people in the lobby. He recognized the very white man among the *policía* and did not like the determined, frightened look on the pale man's pale face.

"I would like to have some words with you."

So this is how it ends? Santiago thought. He said, "What is this that has happened?"

"There has been another abduction," the officer said. "A young woman was attacked and taken from one of the rooms. I would like to discuss this matter with you."

"All right," Santiago said amiably enough. "Would you like I wait in my room?"

"You can wait here, please," the officer said, and that was when the very white man began shouting, shouting and pointing, and all of the officers and many of the monks and patrons who had gathered in the lobby all turned to look, and their eyes all came to rest on Pablo Santiago. Devout groundskeeper Santiago.

Although they all stared, no one — not even the police — seemed to understand what they were staring at until the very white man, in a hoarse and strained voice, shouted, "That shoe! That shoe! This is my Isabel's shoe!"

So Pablo Santiago followed their eyes and looked down and, sure enough, the woman's missing shoe had somehow managed to hook itself into one of the many loops of Santiago's work belt.

"Well," Santiago said, "I suppose you have found what you have found."

Chief of Police Tomás Barrera, looking quite dark and young and upset, entered the interrogation room and sat down at the table opposite Pablo Santiago. Santiago, in cuffs, looked up from the tabletop and smiled at Tomás Barrera.

"Your father and I," Santiago said, "we grew up on this land together. Your father was a good man, Tomás. I miss him now that he is dead."

"Mr. Santiago," Tomás Barrera began, "I have my men down

at the car now. They have opened the trunk and they have started digging in the flats for the bodies. You have cooperated thus far, Mr. Santiago, and it may do you more good to cooperate further."

"I have told you," Santiago said, "I refuse to go back there. You have caught me and I have given up my God, but I cannot go back there and I will not show you the bodies. I have explained where they are buried and if your men are good diggers and hard workers, they will find them all."

"And how many will we find, Mr. Santiago?"

"*Seis.*"

"English, please," said Tomás Barrera. "This is not Mexico."

"Six," Santiago repeated. He did not tell the young officer that he was uncertain about the number.

"Why did you do this?"

"I have come to know things," Santiago said. "That is why."

"What do you know?" Tomás Barrera said.

"What I have found."

"And what have you found, Mr. Santiago?"

"*El Dios,*" said Santiago. "God."

"Is that so?"

"I have learned," Santiago said, "that God is always looking for a way to speak with us, Tomás Barrera. There are many ways but most times, people do not listen. Maybe it is true that I happened to be listening one day, and there is His voice for me to hear. God, He comes in any form, from the burning bush to the modern automobile. We have to be aware, Tomás Barrera. That is all."

"You raped those women and locked them in the trunk," the young officer said.

"It was God's will," Santiago explained. "We are now in preparation for the Second Coming of Christ. He will return as before in the womb of a young woman, a union of human seed and human egg. You do not understand, Tomás Barrera, that it was my job to select all the pretty girls and offer my seed. If it is as it should be, God will take the girl in her pregnancy and raise her in one of the many depths of purgatory. After seven days, God will decide whether He approves of my selection, my donation. He may then take the girl or leave her to die."

"In the trunk of the car," Tomás Barrera finished.

"What is a trunk?" Santiago said. "What is a car?" Clearing his throat, he continued, "Unfortunately, He has yet to approve of my selections. But this last time ..." Santiago's voice rose a notch. "May I ask a question?"

"What is it?"

"When you opened the trunk tonight, what did you find?"

"I think you know what we found."

"I do not," said Santiago. "Do you not understand the words I've just spoken?"

"Isabel Fitzgerald was in the trunk, Mr. Santiago," Tomás Barrera said. "She was in the trunk dead and raped and half-frozen."

"Oh." There was no expression on Santiago's face. "She died quick. Was it the head injury?"

"Asphyxiation. She suffocated in the trunk."

"Well," Santiago said with mild interest, "that had never occurred to me."

Tomás Barrera stood and moved toward the door.

"Wait," Santiago said, and the young officer paused. "You must keep her in the trunk undisturbed for seven days. She is the one and the mission has been completed. You cannot remove her, or this will have to be done all over again."

"She has been removed," Tomás Barrera said coldly. "Anything else?"

"No," Pablo Santiago said, looking back down at the table. "Except, this has been most ignoble for me. Sitting here like this with chains on my wrists ..." Santiago's eyes unfocused and for a moment it looked as though he had fallen into a deep sleep. Then, before Tomás Barrera could leave the room, Santiago said, "Yes, I think it would have been much better to go over the cliff like the black bear. Don't you agree?"

Tomás Barrera said nothing.

Cold, dark, late, and Chief of Police Tomás Barrera walked along the sandstone flat high above the canyon. Above him burned high-intensity fluorescent lights, stretching his shadow out along the scrub land and over the edge of the cliff. Around him, many men worked with high-powered drilling equipment to exhume Pablo Santiago's victims.

Finishing a cigarette, Barrera approached Officer Andy Lopez, who was crouched on his hams with a flashlight peering into one of the shallow graves.

"How many we got so far?" Barrera asked.

"Well, either Santiago was lying or just couldn't remember, but we got about seventeen corpses so far. All young girls."

Barrera thought he misheard the man. "For serious?"

"This summer only about three girls have gone missing, two of which were staying at the monastery. All these other girls — Christ, the guy must have been traveling and picking them up across the state."

"Seventeen?" Barrera heard himself repeat.

"What a mess," Officer Lopez muttered.

Slipping his hands inside his nylon coat, Barrera trudged through the underbrush back toward the highway, breathing in the cool, crisp night air. The dark, swarthy shape of the Mercury Comet, half-hidden in a copse of firs, caught his attention, and he headed over to it. Ran two fingers across its hood. Tomorrow morning, he would have a truck sent from the city to haul the thing away. *How in the world did you even get here?* he wondered, moving around to the driver's door. Cupping his hands about his face, he peered through the filthy glass into the car. With one hand he opened the door ... and caught a whiff of ancient soil and blood and something stronger, more pungent, that reminded him of barnyards and cow shit.

Carefully, delicately, Tomás Barrera entered the vehicle and situated himself behind the steering wheel. He fingered the steering column, the horn ring, ran his palm along the dusty lip of the dashboard. Looking down, he noticed the radio dial beside his right knee. He jiggled the knobs, turning them, spinning the dial. Smiled. His father used to have a car like this. Not a Comet, but an old Mustang. And weren't all those old cars the same, anyway?

Officer Lopez turned his flashlight on Barrera's face. Wincing, Barrera waved him away.

"You been in there for over an hour," Lopez said. "Want me to call your wife and tell her you moved out?"

"Over an hour?" Barrera muttered. "What time is it?"

"After midnight."

"Jesus Christ."

"Something wrong, Chief?"

After a moment, Tomás Barrera shook his head and climbed out of the car. A weak sigh escaped him when Lopez slammed the door shut.

"One hell of a mess," Lopez said, hands on his hips. He was looking out over the darkened rim of the canyon. Below, the rush of the river was easily heard. "You want I should get a tow-truck up here to take this piece of junk away?"

"No," Barrera said, and he thought the words came from his mouth too quickly. "Don't worry about it, I'll take care of it."

Officer Andy Lopez shrugged. "Suit yourself," he said, and headed through the ponderosa pines in the direction of the highway.

MOVING PICTURES
by Gord Rollo

The first punch stunned the tall skinny man, snapping his head back violently. It knocked him away from the door he'd been pathetically attempting to block, and allowed Ronnie to enter the room unimpeded. Blood flowed freely from the shopkeeper's lip, and a few tears trickled out of his downcast eyes, but he made no cry of pain. No protest whatsoever. This disappointed Ronnie. He preferred it when they screamed.

"You owe me five hundred bucks, Stretch. Cough it up ... or pay the price. Your choice. I ain't got all night."

"I d-d-don't have it," the tall man stuttered; his quavering voice revealed that he was either scared — or more likely — lying.

Ronnie smiled, cracked his knuckles, and balled his hands into fists. This might get interesting after all, he thought.

***

Having finished collecting from all eight storeowners in less than an hour, the four thousand dollars tucked safely away, Ronnie turned up his collar and headed for home. They were calling for a thunderstorm and he didn't want to get caught out in that. He didn't have to drop off the cash until morning, so there was no reason to stand around and freeze his butt off.

This was Ronnie's new job. He was a "rent" collector, which was a step up from his last job driving the boss' mother-in-law around the city, shopping day after day. Ronnie wasn't the big hulking bruiser people normally associated with this line of work, but he didn't exactly look like a choirboy either. He was a big guy with thick dark hair and even darker eyes, six feet two, and just shy of two hundred pounds. With his leather jacket, he liked to think he looked like a muscular version of Brando in *The Wild Bunch*. What he lacked in brute strength, he more than made up for in sheer cruelty. The only problem with his new job was how things were proving to be *too* easy. So far, all he'd had to do was mention he was sent by the family and the storeowners literally jumped to attention, handing over the cash. He was all gung-ho to kick some ass, but only that one tall skinny guy with the stutter had tried giving him a hard time. Even there, it had only taken a punch to get inside his shop and one more to the ribs to make him change his tune about not having any money.

Oh well. At least his boss was letting him handle money again. That meant he'd earned his reputation back. If he didn't fuck this up, things might start to look up after all.

He'd only taken a dozen steps, when he spotted the small sign displayed in the front window of previously abandoned convenience store. Ronnie hadn't noticed the sign on his first sweep down the block, being preoccupied with collecting from the names on his list. In neatly printed red paint, it said:

MOVING PICTURES
Tattoos so beautiful — they'll move your soul!

Opening Soon

What the hell is this, Ronnie thought. Somebody's opening up a new store ... a tattoo joint!

This was just his luck. Things had gone great that night, now here was this new store to throw a wrench in his cushy new job. The eight old owners were broken down and submissive before he'd even knocked on a single door, but this new guy might not be so complacent. Christ, it was a tattoo parlor. What if the owner was some three-hundred pound ex-biker with arms as big around as his head? What if he smiled and said, "Fuck you" to Ronnie's threats?

Of course, there was a flip side as well. There was every

chance the new owner would just hand over the cash, preferring to be left alone, rather than hassled. If that happened, and Ronnie was to hand over forty-five hundred bucks to his boss, with a story about how he muscled a new faithful customer, he might come out of this smelling pretty damn sweet.

There was only one way to find out, so Ronnie walked over and rapped on the door as loud as he could, and continued pounding until a light came on in the apartment upstairs. Any fears of an enormous pissed-off biker vanished instantly when Ronnie saw who finally opened the door. It was a small, frail-looking Oriental man gazing back at him with frightened eyes. He was old, with an incredibly wrinkled face beneath brush-cut gray hair. He was wearing a long, slightly stained white undershirt that hung just below his skinny trembling knees.

"Wha — what you want?" the old man asked. "Please, you go away now. No open door after dark. Come back in daytime, okay?"

Ronnie liked the way he pleaded. He liked it a lot. This old man wasn't going to give him any trouble, or at least he'd better not if he knew what was good for him.

"You owe me money, old man," Ronnie snarled, easily slipping into his tough guy routine, the threat of violence seeping out with every word.

"What? Money? No-no-no, you wrong mister. I no owe you money. I no owe money to anyone."

"You calling me a liar, Chinky?" Ronnie hissed, shoving his way inside the store, slapping the old man hard on his right cheek.

"Ahh! No, please. No calling liar. Just mistake, that's all. Please, you leave now. I no owe money. I just starting up business here. I very good artist, make good tattoos."

Ronnie ignored him, brushing him aside to wander around the place. "Nice set up the have here, Chinky … real nice. Be a shame if you weren't able to open up your business on account of someone wrecking the place, wouldn't it?"

Ronnie hurled an empty ceramic bowl, shattering it against the wall for emphasis. That captured the old man's attention and he proceeded to fill the tattoo artist in on how the protection game worked down on Market Street. One more tipped over desk and a couple more slaps, and Ronnie had finished his speech.

"So be a good boy, Chinky, be a smart boy, and hand over the fucking money."

A steely defiance shone from the old man's sad eyes and when he spoke, his voice was changed — low, powerful, almost a quiet growl.

"I know how game works, bastard. Same game made me lose last business over on West Lincoln Street. Those animals — maybe friends of yours, huh — stole eight hundred off me every month. Damn them and damn you, I not pay you single penny. Get out!"

"Easy now Chinky, you don't want to be taking that tone of voice with me. I just might take offense, dig?"

The Chinese storeowner never answered, choosing to remain quiet, rigid and defiant.

"You some kind of tough guy?" Ronnie asked, viciously poking the old man with his finger, puffing up his chest to appear as large and menacing as possible.

"No, not tough guy. Just honest old man trying hard to make living. It hard with people like you around."

"That's a real touching story," Ronnie laughed, "but you better understand that I don't give a shit. I want my money Chinky, and I want it now. Think of the money you're saving. That last guy wanted eight hundred bucks and I only want five. That's three big bills you get to keep each month — hell, I'm letting you off easy."

The Chinese storeowner slumped down onto a creaky wooden chair, emotions raging inside of him as he pondered his limited options. Ronnie let him think about it for a minute, confident the old man would make the smart choice and pay up. He was surprised when the tattoo artist looked up and quietly answered, "This happen to me too many times. It happen no more. I pay you nothing."

Ronnie smiled at him, a sadistic leering smile that said he'd been hoping the old man would say that. He was determined to get the money, even if it meant beating the stuffing out of the old goat every month to do it. It might even be fun. Now was as good a time as any to hand out the first beating — and Ronnie was prepared to do just that — when a small child surprised him by walking into the room. It was a boy, about eight or nine years old, whose glance flickered back and forth between Ronnie and the tattoo artist.

"What's the matter, Grandpa? I heard loud noises and shouting. Is everything okay?"

"Yes child, everything fine," the old man answered. "Please, go back to room now."

His voice remained neutral, but by the fear shining in his eyes, it was clear he was far more worried and anxious than he'd been a few minutes ago. And Ronnie knew why. It was the boy, his grandchild. He'd resigned himself to the fact that Ronnie was going to rough him up, but he was clearly terrified at the thought of Ronnie hurting the child. Ronnie read the old man's fear, and quickly used it to his advantage.

"It's okay, little guy", he walked over and gently brushed the dark hair out of his sleepy eyes. "There's no problem here." Then still keeping a hold of him by the back of his fragile neck, he turned to the tattoo artist, saying, "Right, Chinky? No problem here at all. Or is there?"

The threat was impossible to miss, the weight of it striking the old man worse than any physical blow.

"The choice is yours, little man. Pay up ... or live with the consequences."

The tattoo artist let out a weary sigh and slumped even farther down onto the wooden chair. A single tear balled up on his right eyelash, then tumbled down his wrinkled cheek to the corner of his tightly pursed lips.

"I pay you ... I pay. Just no hurt child, he all I have."

"Smart choice, Chinky," Ronnie said, allowing the frightened child to head back upstairs to bed. "Well then, now that we have an understanding, if you just hand over the cash I'll be glad to get out of your —"

"I no have the five hundred dollars," the old man cut him off. "I no have anything right now. I not even opened yet. No make any cash yet. Please, I pay, just need a few weeks."

Unlike the stuttering man, Ronnie believed him. Odds were he was telling the truth; the fear in his eyes over his grandchild's safety too great for him to risk lying. No big deal, Ronnie thought to himself. His boss wasn't even aware of the new business. What harm would it do to cut the old bugger a break and stall for a few weeks? Besides, if he did lay a beating on him, he'd be unable to open up his shop, and then he'd never get the money. Ronnie was just about to agree to the deal, when the Chinese man spoke first.

"How 'bout I give you something now as down payment? No cash, but something beautiful. Valuable too."

Ronnie had long since learned to take whatever you could get your hands on. If someone wanted to make you an offer, you listened carefully and took anything that was free.

"I'm listening. What have you got?"

"Tattoo."

"What are you talking about?"

"Tattoo. I give you beautiful tattoo. Anything you want. I real good artist. My tattoos worth lots of money — two hundred, two hundred fifty dollars."

"Two hundred ... you're crazy. I can get a tattoo done for fifty or sixty bucks."

"Not like my tattoos. Come look, please."

The small man led Ronnie to the back wall of the store, where literally hundreds of colorful sketches were on display, each neatly thumb-tacked to the paneling. The old man hadn't lied. He was an exceptional artist, brilliant in fact. His sketches were so vivid and detailed, so dazzling and colorful.

"Hey man, these *are* fantastic," Ronnie said, temporarily forgetting why he was there.

"Yes. You see, in China, tattoo sacred. It not the long-haired motorcycle gang, trace-the-lines parlors that all over this country. No. Back home, it still regarded as rare form of Art, unique because the artist uses the living canvas for his work. Tattoo honorable skill, passed down father to son, generation to generation. My son die, but I teach the boy, my grandchild, to someday take my place. I train many years to perfect my art. Worth lots of money, yes? Now I give to you, free. You pick one

… okay?"

Ronnie had secretly always wanted a tattoo, figuring it would make him look all the tougher. The only reason he didn't already have one was because in all the places he'd visited, the tattoos had looked stupid — more cartoonish than art. Not here though, this old man's work was outstanding.

"Okay Chinky, you got yourself a deal, but the tattoo only buys you two weeks. After that, I'll be back for my money. Got it?"

The old man nodded once, and said, "Choose then," sweeping his wrinkled hand along the wall of sketches.

After ten minutes of scanning the wall, Ronnie finally decided on the big, fiery-red scorpion. There was just something about the way it held its head up high, proud and majestic, and carried its long, lethal-spiked tail low, subtle yet lethally threatening. The others were brilliant, but no matter how many times he rechecked the wall, he kept returning to the crimson scorpion. It was definitely the one.

"That's the one," Ronnie pointed. "I want it on my left arm."

"As you wish," the frail artist bowed, exiting the room for a moment before returning with his tools and a tray of powdered ink.

"We begin now," he said.

Ronnie watched with a mixture of disbelief and fascination, as the little man knelt on the floor and began chanting in a strange language, his hands clenched tightly in front of his heart in prayer. He droned on for several minutes before beginning the process of carefully, almost reverently, mixing the powdered inks with an amber-colored fluid poured from a black ceramic flask. When everything was ready, the aged artist dipped a finger in the red ink bowl, smeared a crimson X on his forehead and rose to his feet to begin.

Fucking weird, Ronnie thought, but kept his opinion to himself. Some things were better left unsaid.

It took longer than Ronnie expected, nearly two full hours, and hurt like hell. The pain had been unbearable at first, like putting your arm under a sowing machine or sticking it into a hive filled with angry bees. Thankfully his arm went numb after a few minutes, the pain settling out into a dull throbbing ache — intense but tolerable. Barely.

When the old man was finished, he handed Ronnie a large hand held mirror to inspect his work. Ronnie gasped. Holy Shit, he thought. It was by far the most beautiful thing he had ever seen, looking even more vivid and colorful on his arm than in the wall sketch. More than satisfied, Ronnie hurried home to his apartment, not even bothering to threaten the talented artist on his way out. The little bugger was smart enough to know he'd come back to collect the money — free tattoo or not.

A good night's work complete, Ronnie relaxed for a while on his worn sofa with a cold beer, returning to the bathroom mirror numerous times to admire his tattoo before heading off to bed a happy man. His new job was a piece of cake, he was going to make some decent money again, and maybe — just maybe — he'd still make something of himself after all. He fell asleep almost immediately, a huge grin spread across his face for the first time in years.

***

A sharp crack of thunder jolted Ronnie out of a troubled sleep; he'd been dreaming of something monstrous stalking him through dimly lit, narrow corridors. He'd never actually seen what had been following him, but he could vividly recall the terror in his heart as he ran for his life. The childish nightmare frightened him more than he cared to admit. Ronnie's heart was racing; his body glistened with sweat as he lay in bed catching his breath, and listened to the light pitter-patter of rain falling on the roof. His bedside clock cast an azure-blue aura around the shadow-shrouded room, its glowing numbers indicating 3:24 a.m.

Just a stupid dream, he thought, clawing free of the tangled sheets to go take a piss.

Ronnie flushed the toilet then filled the sink with ice cold water. He lowered his head down into it, using his hands to sweep the frigid water over his hair and neck. While submerged,

Ronnie suddenly panicked, seized by the most powerful feeling that someone was in the small bathroom with him, standing right behind him, close enough to reach out…

"Ahhh … hemm … urp!" He half screamed, half choked as he launched himself upright and spun around to confront whoever was creeping up behind him.

Ronnie threw two savage punches into the air, before finally managing to wipe the water from his eyes and realize no one was there. He was alone in the cramped room, but he made a point of peeking behind the shower curtain before dropping his guard, lowering his fists. He might have laughed at his absurd reaction, but it had all been so intense, so damn *real*. The nightmare had been scary but easy to understand. This, though, wasn't so simple to shrug off. Ronnie wasn't exactly the type of guy who jumped at shadows, and the events of the last half-hour had left him drained, confused and on edge. What the hell was the matter with him? Why was he so damn spooked?

Pain in Ronnie's left shoulder derailed that particular train of thought, his arm throbbing from the assault of countless tattoo needles, and his needless panic-driven exertions. He moved back to the sink and downed a few Tylenol extra-strength to dull the pain, admiring his tattoo in the mirror as he washed down the tablets with a drink. Something didn't seem right. The blazing red scorpion still looked brilliantly drawn and flawlessly crafted, but something about it seemed, well, different.

"Stop it, man," Ronnie scolded himself, too sore and weary to worry about anything else. "Just get your ass to bed."

Back under the sheets, listening to the rain against the roof again, sleep was a long time coming. Ronnie was exhausted, but found it difficult to settle down. He was just on the verge of drifting off when a strange thought entered his head. It was about his new tattoo, about what had seemed different back in the bathroom.

The scorpion isn't in the same spot. It's up my arm, about an inch closer to my shoulder …

It was a crazy thought, but not crazy enough to keep him awake, slithering into his subconscious with him as he slumbered, coloring his dreams for the rest of the night. Once again, Ronnie was pursued down a dimly lit paneled corridor, but this time his terror-stricken mind knew exactly what relentlessly gave chase.

***

The storm was gone by morning, the sun's golden rays streaming in through Ronnie's bedroom window, warming his face and penetrating his closed eyelids enough to wake him up. Ronnie squinted into the bright light, rolled away from it onto his sore arm. The pain made Ronnie remember his nightmares and his strange thought about his tattoo not being where he'd remembered it. It was all nonsense, of course, totally ridiculous when he stopped to really think about it. How could a tattoo possibly move?

Still, he checked his arm in the mirror anyway, laughing at his childish fears, making fun of himself in spite of how real it had seemed in the middle of the night. In the bright light of day, it was far easier to laugh it off as the silly ravings of an exhausted half-asleep mind. The scorpion was right where it was supposed to be, right where the old Chinese artist had ...

... Ronnie's smile fell off his face like an outcropping of ice dropping from the edge of a glacier into the cold dark sea.

Was it up that high on my arm yesterday? I thought I asked the Chinaman to —

"For fuck's sake. Get a grip, man," Ronnie shouted at his pale reflection. "They put people away who talk like that."

He pondered the crimson artwork on his arm for a few more seconds. Then, shaking his head at his crazy thoughts, pulled on a clean white T-shirt and went to finish getting dressed. He didn't have time to play "Who Wants To Go Bonkers Today?" with himself. It was almost ten o'clock. He had to get his ass in gear and deliver the four grand he'd collected last night. Jake would be starting to wonder where he was soon, and the last thing Ronnie needed was Jake mad at him. He was dressed and out the door in a flash.

It was a magnificent morning, what with the warm sun, the clear blue sky, and the fresh smell of the city that only happened after a good cleansing rainstorm. The walk did Ronnie good, cleared the cobwebs out of his head. He quickly forgot about his tattoo. In fact, he never thought of it again until he'd delivered Jake his cash and was telling him and a few of the boys about how a new storeowner was opening up on Market Street. He told them what had happened, playing up how he'd strong-armed the owner into giving him a free tattoo.

Jake seemed real happy with Ronnie's slightly exaggerated story and slipped him an extra hundred dollars for drumming up new business.

"Good work Ron, I'm proud of you." Jake slapped him on the back. "Well, let's see it then."

"See what?" Ronnie asked, then realized his boss wanted to check out his tattoo. He pulled up the sleeve of his T-shirt an inch or two, proudly letting the boys in the room get an eyeful. "What do ya think? Not too shabby, huh?"

Nobody said a word. Everyone looked at Ronnie strange, as if he'd grown two heads or something.

"Stop fucking around, Ron," Jake said, "Show us the tattoo, for Christ's sake."

Ronnie's cocky attitude wilted and died, fear literally squeezing the breath from his lungs, like a hug from a world record Boa Constrictor. He didn't want to, didn't think he was *able* to, but somehow, he found the courage to glance down at his exposed arm, seeing but not quite believing there was nothing to look at except smooth white skin. Ronnie's legs threatened to buckle, his stomach clenched and spasmed. He would have vomited right there and then, if he'd remembered to eat breakfast that morning.

What the fuck is going on? It can't be gone ... it just can't!

It wasn't.

When Ronnie tugged his shirt up another few inches, there the scorpion was, engraved into his skin in all its crimson glory as always. Only this time there was no doubt whatsoever — Ronnie's tattoo had impossibly, incomprehensibly, moved to the curve of his shoulder, moved at least four inches up his arm from the spot it had originally been needled into his flesh.

***

He ran home from Jake's office in a state of semi-shock, his panic escalating, his confused mind spinning in all directions at once. Inside his apartment, Ronnie dashed to the bathroom mirror, crying out in horror when he learned that the scorpion tattoo had moved again, cresting his left shoulder to sit at the apex of his collarbone.

It's going for my throat! Ronnie's mind coldly calculated, a shiver running through his entire body at the bizarre thought.

Fear can do amazing things to someone's normal way of thinking, make them do crazy things they'd never usually consider, and Ronnie had never been so scared in his entire life. His cloudy mind decided that he had to get the *thing* off of his body, and get it off fast before it inched its way any closer to his neck. The scorpion was going to kill him if he didn't do something right away. From the kitchen, he picked up a sharp paring knife, slicing into the meat of his arm, trying to carve the tattoo from his shoulder.

"I have to get this fucking thing off me!" he shrieked, blind panic giving rent to an act of sheer madness.

There was only one way Ronnie's confused mind could think of to accomplish the task. To guarantee success, he would have to cut his whole arm off. It was irrational, insane even, but he couldn't think of any other way to get rid of the crimson scorpion.

He owned a big fishing knife. He kept it in a rusty tackle box on a shelf in the spare bedroom closet. Minutes later he'd gathered it, washed it under scalding soapy water, and prepared to make his cut.

The serrated edge was warm to the touch as Ronnie pumped himself up, trying to work up the courage to do what he intended. He aimed the blade just in front of the menacing scorpion's outstretched front claws, gritted his broken teeth again, and began sawing savagely into his own shoulder before his resolve weakened. White-hot pain lanced cruelly into Ronnie's brain, dark red rivers of blood gushed over his fingers and ran in streaks down his chest and back. It was agony personified, every fiber in his nervous system begged for release, but Ronnie determined to carry on. And he would have too, but the fillet knife stopped when he had only cut down half an inch, steel grinding to a halt on the beige-colored knob of his exposed collarbone.

Reality broke through Ronnie's thin veneer of madness, clearing his mind long enough to allow him to see the futility of his masochistic efforts. He was never going to be able to cut off his own arm, not with a fishing knife in any case. He'd need a hatchet, or maybe an axe, but even then Ronnie seriously doubted he'd have the ability or the fortitude to finish the job. His arm shredded, bloodied and hanging uselessly at his side, Ronnie slumped down at the kitchen table, rested his feverish head in his right palm, and wept like a baby.

The more Ronnie thought it over, the more he was convinced the tattoo artist was responsible — who else could have done this to him? Why hadn't he realized it before? In all the mayhem, he'd been either too mired in denial or madness or both to stop and think about it. Then he did though, thought long and hard about it, and soon knew exactly where he had to go next, and what he had to do once he got there. Cursing the Chinaman under his breath, Ronnie grabbed his Marlon Brando jacket, picked up the bloodstained filleting knife and ran for the front door.

**

Market Street ran East to West, bisecting Talbot Avenue where Ronnie lived, twelve city blocks to the south of his apartment. He sprinted there like a man possessed, a nightmare covered in blood and black leather, running until he stood in front of the Chinaman's shop.

MOVING PICTURES
Tattoos so beautiful — they'll move your soul!
Opening Soon

"Not if I have anything to say about it, it won't," Ronnie

hissed, and charged into the store.

He skidded to a stop, two steps inside the store, his bravado fading, his thundering heart leapt into his throat. Not ten feet away the aged Chinaman sat cross-legged on the floor, his arms folded regally in front of his puffed out chest. Wearing a stunning crimson colored silk robe with a gold sash tightly binding it around his waist, he no longer resembled the frail little man Ronnie remembered shoving around the previous night. He was larger somehow, emanating a cold menacing aura of great power.

"I've been expecting you," the robed man quietly spoke, all his charade dropped, his poor man's broken English no longer needed. "Kneel before me, and there's a chance you might yet live."

Ronnie wanted to charge at the frail man, cut him into tiny wrinkled up pieces, or beat the life out of him with his bare hands, but he hesitated, unsure what was happening, resisting the anger that might get him killed. If the Chinaman said there was a way out of this mess, he'd be a fool not to listen. Ronnie did as he was instructed, walking forward and kneeling in front of the mysterious shopkeeper.

"What — what the hell is going on here, Chinky?" Ronnie asked, too confused and light-headed from loss of blood to notice the insulting way he'd addressed the man before him.

"My name is Jung Tao Chiang," the robed man thundered, his powerful booming voice rattling the ceramic bowls half way across the room. "Understand something. Your life hangs by the thinnest of threads." Handing Ronnie an elaborately designed golden mirror from a deep pocket in his robe, he said, "Here. See for yourself how close the Reaper stands."

Ronnie took the mirror, and with shaking hands brought it up to his throat to see what he already half suspected. His throat had turned red, the crimson scorpion now tattooed onto the left side of his neck, its powerful tail arched above its head, its deadly stinger coiled and ready to strike.

"I suggest you sit real still," the tattoo artist said with an icy grin, "and listen carefully to what I have to say. Understand?"

Ronnie could only nod, not wanting to risk speaking and disturbing the monstrosity that had somehow fused to his skin.

"Okay then, where should I start? As I said, my name is Jung Tao Chiang, and I wasn't lying to you when I told you my artwork was very rare. I am one of only a handful of people still alive, skilled in the art of Chaon Li. There is no literal translation into English, but Living Pictures or Moving Pictures will suffice.

"I could explain it to you all day and you still wouldn't understand, but in simple terms, I am a magician, an enchanter who can summon forth minor deities from other planes of existence, bringing them here under my control."

If Ronnie weren't so terrified, he'd have laughed in the Chinaman's face. Had he really said *deities*? What the hell was he babbling about? As it was, he kept his mouth shut, smartly realizing there was no intended humor in what the Chinaman was saying.

"In ancient times, Chaon Li artists would be brought in and paid handsomely to call forth an entity capable of bringing good luck or health and prosperity to the homeowner, or shopkeeper, or whoever. In times of trouble, an overseer, a protector could be called on to watch over children, or wives, or valuable livestock. They could also be used to seek out enemies and strike them down when they least expect it."

"Nowadays, unknown to most of my paying customers, I give them a *Shanoa Che*, a simple pixie that can bring good luck. Others, those in the know who require something more powerful, travel from all over the world to seek me out. These living pictures could be drawn anywhere, any shape, any size, a colorful picture on a wall, a design on the bedroom floor … or hidden within the beauty of a tattoo. Understand? You, my friend … you happen to have a very powerful *Itren Hian*, a protector demon resting half an inch from your jugular vein. Mark my words. It will strike if you do not do exactly as I ask."

Ronnie's mouth had suddenly gone dry. He was scared, but the weight of the filleting knife hid in his coat pocket. If he got the chance, and he'd only need a few seconds, he wouldn't hesitate to use it.

"What, hmm, what do you want from me? I never did anything to you. I was just doing what I was told, doing my job."

"Exactly … and that's what I want you to keep on doing. If I kill you, this extortion racket won't go away. Your pitiful boss will just hire another thug and start over. It's always the same. I had to kill three collectors over on West Lincoln before they finally got the message and left me alone.

"You will pay my five hundred protection money, how is of no concern to me. You'll pay so your boss thinks I'm being a good little storeowner and I can be left in peace. In return, you get to live, and I make the protector on you neck return to its rightful spot on your arm. It won't go away, of course, but won't harm you either … unless you try and cross me. Here, take another look."

Ronnie raised the golden mirror to his throat again, and was greatly relieved to see that the scorpion was no longer there. He would have liked to take off his jacket to see if his tattoo had indeed returned to his arm, but he didn't want the Chinaman to see the handle of his knife concealed in his inside coat pocket.

This was the break Ronnie had been waiting for, a mistake on the tattoo artist's part by moving the scorpion out of striking distance, even if it would only be for a moment. With no time to spare, and no intention of ever becoming the weird little freak's private slave, Ronnie lashed out. He leapt to his feet, grabbing for, withdrawing, and lunging with the knife with a lightning quick practiced flair. He'd drop the sucker dead long before —

— The razor sharp tip of the scorpion's stinger plunged into the tender flesh of Ronnie's throat, gouging an inch deep hole in his jugular. Blood spurted across the ceiling in a wide arc as if a ketchup bottle had exploded. Potent venom shot through Ronnie's body, riding the red liquid highway from his neck wound straight to his heart. Within an instant, an incredible heat enveloped Ronnie's body, searing out any pain, boiling his brain in its own juices as he collapsed to the floor, his arms and legs already twitching and stiffening to uselessness.

"Stupid fool," the tattoo artist muttered. "I gave you a chance and you wasted it. Now you pay the price."

Ronnie heard him speak, heard the words ringing in his ears as if coming from a great distance. He struggled to turn over onto his back, to say something, anything, to beg for forgiveness, for help, but that wasn't going to happen. He managed to roll onto his right side, but that was as far as he would ever get. He felt a little tickle on his neck, and watched in wonder through rapidly dimming eyes, as a real flesh and blood scorpion lurched slowly past his face. It paused to turn and gaze at him, and then turned to greet its master. The crimson robed old man got down on his knees beside the scorpion, bowed, and spoke to it in that strange chanting language Ronnie couldn't understand. The scorpion seemed to nod its head, then, its task completed, crumbled into a pile of powdered red ink right in front of Ronnie Marchelli's eyes. He might have been surprised, even astonished, but he was already dead.

THE ESSENCES
by Davin Ireland

The tall man in the cashmere overcoat tottered into the alley around noon, bumped a wall hard enough to dislodge some of the snow that clung to his broad, stooping shoulders, and proceeded to describe a ragged circle among the frozen dog turds.

Immediately my body contracted into a hard ball amid the refuse that surrounded me. This wasn't part of the script. Cousin Luigi's was expecting a seafood delivery around one; a few minutes after that, the shipping clerk at Drago Dynamics would be cutting through this way on his daily shuttle-run to the bagel shop over on Westfield Avenue. Nobody had mentioned a walk-on. Not to me. Hand straying to the weapon scotch-taped to my upper thigh, I waited to see if the intrusion was accidental or staged.

"Eyrie, this is Gem," I whispered into my straggling beard, "I have a Caucasian male, six-four, mid- to late-forties directly in front of me?"

I phrased the report like a question so that the boys in the Eyrie — our name for the top-floor office coordinating this entire operation — would know not to screw about asking dumb questions. If the situation was critical, I needed to know right away.

"Copy that, Gem," uttered a tinny voice in my ear, "not one of ours. Are you in need of assistance?"

For no good reason I found myself hesitating. The figure in the overcoat, obviously plenty the worse for wear, was at least a head taller than me and a couple of stone heavier. But these weren't punch-bag pounds I was looking at. Even from back here in the dumpster, which stank so bad it made my eyes water just to breathe its fetid air, I could see my visitor was seriously out of shape. Face alcohol-fattened, skin pale and loose around the jowls, he'd definitely seen better days. But it was the eyes that did it for me. Down-turned and shimmering, as if they were about to liquefy and run down his cheeks. This was a man haunted by visions most of us can scarcely even dream of.

"No assistance as of yet," I countered, and hauled myself across a mound of decomposing garbage. Not a good idea. Even though my movements were scant, the disturbance was enough to release a moist, vile-smelling stench from beneath me. For the next few seconds my curses rang through the Eyrie like rusty chimes through a churchyard. I don't know how often I'd asked for an empty dumpster to be placed out there beside the overflowing ones, but I know exactly how often I'd been refused: every single time. The brass reckoned this stage of the operation was so delicate that any deviation from the norm, including the amount of waste produced by the adjacent restaurants, might be enough to frighten off our quarry.

I bet the suits'd whistle another tune if *they* were the ones up to their elbows in orange peel and coffee grinds at all hours of the day and night. I was about to go winging off on another mental rant concerning department mismanagement — a common theme of late — when my friend in the cashmere, having made erratic progress towards my position, drew his last breath. There was nothing spectacular about it. One minute he was listing between the two buildings like a drunk on a four-day bender, the next he had fallen flat on his face with a resounding smack.

Fearing that our operation was about to be compromised, I unclipped my surveillance mike, which had been woven directly into my beard extensions ten days before, vaulted the slippery edge of the dumpster and landed feet-first in a freezing cold puddle of deliquescing slush.

Welcome to the glorious hi-tech world that is insurance fraud investigation.

***

As it turned out, the dead guy's name was Victor Mortenson. Whilst still in the upright position and inhaling oxygen, he had worked as a corporate strategist for a large multi-national located just south of the river. Freshly deceased he was survived by a wife, three kids, and an exemplary taste in music (the Discman in his breast pocket was paused on track five of Steely Dan's outstanding *Pretzel Logic* album). Mortenson was also known to have frequented Blockbuster Video on Sandmoor Street, N16, in his spare time. Judging by the various other odds and ends I retrieved from his wallet, he hadn't been adverse to spending money, either. Credit cards, debit cards, banker's drafts, cheque books; this was one high-rolling corpse.

I checked for signs of a pulse one last time, then decided to kick it upstairs. The thing that stopped me was Mortenson's tightly-clenched fist. It looked like it meant something. I forced the whitened fingers apart, just managing to prise loose a folded scrap of paper no larger than a Post-It note. In fact, it *was* a Post-It note. On one side was scribbled a name and a location: *Jacob Legrash, 13th Floor, Temple Towers building* — with beneath that a street address scrawled in a different colour ink. On the other, printed in letters so small I had to squint to read them, the bewildering postscript: *Keeper of the Essences.*

I turned Mortenson over and thumbed his eyelids. Instead of the usual scarlet filaments edging the outer rim of the cornea, most of the surface capillaries appeared bluish-grey and horribly calcified. On top of that, the throat, which had only looked flabby before, bulged against the button-down collar in a way I didn't like at all. I hadn't considered the cause of death up until that point. A drugs overdose would probably have topped my list, with poisoning — possibly alcohol-related — a close second. But this nasty little brace of symptoms put me more in mind of a tropical disease.

"Gem, are you in trouble?"

It was Kirkland from upstairs, stressing into my earpiece. I stowed the slip of paper in my pocket and retrieved the discarded microphone which dangled free at waist level.

"Not me, Al," I soothed, "can't say the same for the guy in the cashmere, though. He's lying down here in the alleyway and he's not moving."

"Have you tried CPR?"

I looked at those hideously marbled eyes and shuddered.

"Are you kidding me?"

Kirkland said something unrepeatable under his breath.

"Gem, sit tight, we're bringing you in."

**

The snow had started to drift by the time we shut up shop. Big lazy flakes of it, sculpted and swirled by the wind. Perhaps Mortenson's appearance had been an omen of some sort. At least now I wouldn't freeze to death. Showered, changed and freshly debriefed, I trudged back to the car with no real plans for the day beyond finding myself a nice secluded pub with a blazing hearth and plenty of scalding hot Irish coffee to drink. Instead of that, I locked my dirty laundry in the trunk of my vehicle and kept walking.

There's something strangely redemptive about snow. It covers up the dirt, robs the world of its hard edges, reminds even the most jaded of citizens they were once kids. The only thing it reminded *me* of, unfortunately, was how poor I had become. With the operation cancelled, our quarry — a City banker suspected of faking his own death to the tune of 1.2 million quid — was free to slip into obscurity forever. That meant we were going to take a bath. When your cut is forty percent of all funds recovered, you tend not to skimp on the details. Man power, office space, equipment rental — that's a lot of money when you've got nothing coming in at the end of the day.

These thoughts, and many others like them, haunted my mind as I stalked ever southwards — from Bromley to Poplar and beyond, crossing Aspen Way and the East India Dock Road before finally arriving at the Isle of Dogs. The thing was, I'd withheld the information on the Post-It note from Kirkland on purpose, and had further failed to volunteer same when the woodentops showed up an hour later to take our statements. At first I blamed this lapse in conscience on an oversight, or a reluctance to involve myself further in what was currently a non-paying operation.

But as my destination loomed closer beneath steadily greying skies, I was forced to accept the true nature of my intentions. Victor Mortenson had died clutching a scrap of paper bearing the name of one Jacob Legrash, a man I had neither heard of nor met. It stood to reason that the two men were inextricably linked. And seeing as the former's untimely demise had left me severely out of pocket, one word remained uppermost in my mind.

Reparations.

***

The first thing one notices about Temple Towers is its age. Seeing a peaked slate roof, black-painted brickwork, and overhanging cornices in an area of London that is fast silting up with glass high-rises and shiny steel strutwork, is a bit like finding a roman coin in a handful of plastic poker chips. I approached the front entrance wondering if the place was even occupied. I need not have worried. A pair of charcoal-suited executives vacated the lobby just as I arrived, one of them being kind enough to hold the door for me. I quietly thanked him, and once inside took a moment to compose myself. The next stage was crucial. If I messed this up, I'd either have to accept defeat or get really mercenary about achieving my goals.

I wiped my shoes on the welcome mat and put my best foot forward.

The main hall was tiled checker-board fashion, with plenty of tall ferns in pots to soften the pervading chill in the air. A lone security guard manned a reception desk that was dwarfed by an expressionist oil painting roughly the size of East Grinstead. We established eye contact across about an acre of marble flooring.

"Health and Safety Executive," I announced, once close enough for speech to offer a reasonable alternative to semaphore. "We've had a report concerning your boiler room. Nothing too serious, but it needs checking out." I didn't bother with a 'good morning, sir' or a 'parky out today, guv'. In my experience, the less time you waste on the pleasantries, the more inclined people are to do as you tell them. I selected a fake identity card from the two dozen or so issued to me by the company every January, and handed it over.

"Boiler room," repeated the bemused-looking guard. "You mean the basement?"

"The very same." I perused a list of company names that adorned the wall above a rather sorry looking fax machine, as my bogus credentials were checked. Each name on the list was accompanied by a business logo and a corresponding floor number. There was no number 13, an observation I related to my friend in the peaked cap.

"Well, you know what people are like," he muttered. And when I failed to answer, added: "Unlucky for some?"

"So it does exist," I said. "It's just unoccupied at the moment."

He nodded, a little sheepishly.

With my suspicions confirmed, I flicked through the dialling information on my cellular phone until the number of an ex-girlfriend I'd been meaning to look up for some time popped into view.

"According to the information I have here," I stated, in my most nasal Officialese, "Temple Towers doesn't *have* a thirteenth floor, mister-uh ..."

"Lacey," blustered the security guard, "Stan Lacey." He was getting worried now. Pawing about in an oversized appointments book, waggling his head so that the first signs of a double chin trembled at his jaw-line. He looked on the verge of calling up reinforcements.

"Trust me on this one, Stan," I told him, dropping a note of chummy confidentiality into my voice, "and we'll be able to sort this out among ourselves." I returned my fake ID and cell phone to my jacket and plunged my fists deep into my trouser pockets. It was man-to-man stuff now, strictly off the record. "I believe you do have a thirteenth floor up there," I resumed, "and if you say nobody's collecting on it, that's fine by me. Why should I care? But this is the thing. We both know what happens to unoccupied rental space after a certain amount of time has gone by, don't we? The company on the next floor sanctions a refurbishment and all of its old office furniture ends up getting dumped somewhere out of the way. The tree left over from last year's Christmas party finds its way in there, too. Someone needs a bit of extra room for a stock-take and ends up leaving a few boxes of unwanted files behind ..."

Lacey, who had been nodding in approval from practically the first word, zoned out completely. "Archives," he mumbled, "outdated stock, paperwork left over from bankruptcies. Furniture." He sighed. "It's all up there, all collecting dust. Nobody cares."

"And I dare say most of it is flammable, right? Which according to regulations constitutes a pretty sizeable fire hazard."

When Lacey failed to disagree, I glanced in the direction of the stairs, pretending to make a weighty decision. "So here's what I'm gonna do, Stan. This inspection is A12, which means it's unscheduled. That offers us a little bit of leeway here. If you'd be willing to show me round on thirteen, I'll give your people a week's margin to set the boiler room straight, okay?"

Back in the land of the living, my friend the guard had heard enough. "Take it," he said, producing a key from beneath the reception desk. "Just make sure nobody sees you, okay?"

He got no argument from me.

***

Although my ability to second-guess certain situations has aided me on numerous occasions in the past, precious little of my conversation with security officer Lacey could have prepared me for the overwhelming reality of the thirteenth floor. A vast anachronism against the backdrop of the workaday world, the entire place was crammed floor to ceiling with the junk and refuse (my speciality, it would seem) of decades, much of it antique.

A patina of dust covered everything from filing cabinets to what looked like the sidecar of an old motorcycle — which just for the record was stuffed with mildewed nautical maps rolled into tubes. Standing lamps and coat-trees of all ages and descriptions lined one wall. Art deco coffee tables were stacked by the dozen beside piles of mouldering ledgers, the dates on some of which reached back to the second world war. The atmosphere was stale yet eerily welcoming.

I struck out towards the centre of the floor, navigating between a large leatherette sofa and a defunct printing press that was smeared with oil as black and sticky as congealed blood. There weren't any lights. The fixtures had been removed at some point in the past, and not with any great attention to detail. Electrical cabling spilled from gaps in the ceiling. Fragments of shattered light bulbs crunched underfoot.

I pushed deeper into the gloom, clambering over a century's worth of discarded heritage when the pedestrian route no longer sufficed. I looked from a grimed-in row of windows on one side of the building to a similar row on the other. There were no walls in between: just a series of thick pillars interrupting the view. In the far corner, crouched among the debris of generations, what looked like a knock-together maintenance room was slowly falling to bits. Pieces of broken siding hung loose from nails gone rusty with age. A small rectangle of glass, decorated with a dingy orange curtain, gave the only hint of occupancy.

It was the one place on the entire floor I could conceive of bearing a connection to the mysterious Jacob Legrash. Yet on closer inspection it proved a bitter disappointment. All it contained were a few shelves cluttered with tins of adhesive, the odd jar of screws, and in one corner a two-ring gas stove. Sod it. I was about to call the whole thing off when something creaked beneath my foot. A moment later I was peeling discoloured lino from the floor, heart racing. My instincts were good. Instead of impenetrable concrete, a series of wooden boards housed a trapdoor with a rust-speckled ringbolt at its centre. I felt a rush of adrenalin mingled with a profound sense of confusion. The level of craftsmanship, exhibited by the joins in the wood, suggested the work of a master carpenter or cabinet maker; yet the materials themselves went beyond sub-standard: ancient floorboards, bits of old plywood, splintering planks torn from warehouse pallets, many of which still bore the mark of the manufacturer. No way this stuff had arrived courtesy of a lumber yard. This crap had been scavenged straight from the city dump.

I took hold of the ringbolt and heaved. The trapdoor opened smoothly and soundlessly to reveal a ladder that descended into gloom lit by a single guttering candle stub. The stub sat in a shallow cavity that had been hacked straight into the brickwork. Beyond that, I could see very little. "Anybody down there," I called. "Mr Legrash!"

I didn't expect an answer and none was forthcoming. After all, when you take this much trouble to conceal yourself from the world, acknowledging your whereabouts to the first stranger who comes knocking is hardly likely, is it? And perhaps this wasn't Jacob Legrash to begin with. It could be anyone — a squatter, a former tenant with an axe to grind, a psychotic vagrant who had sneaked into the building's antiquated heating system a generation ago. Well, it was a lot more private than Jubilee Park Tube station, that was for sure. I fingered the slip of paper in my pocket and realised that it didn't matter one way or the other. I had decided to seek out Legrash for reasons of my own, and if the person hiding down there in the darkness was someone else entirely, too bad. I placed my feet on the weathered rungs and commenced my descent.

My first discovery was that this huge, cavernous space — a part of me expected squealing bats and filthy loops of cobweb on the way down — was pleasantly warm and smelt faintly of oleanders. But as a journey of fifteen rungs extended to twenty, then thirty, the atmosphere began to change. Pleasantly warm became oppressively hot, and the faint scent on the air became an overpowering stench.

I was glad to reach the bottom. Abandoning the ladder, I turned full circle, taking in the folly and the grandeur of that magnificent artificial cavern. Not quite a venue in which one might expect to encounter stalactites and burning torches, but not that far from it, either. And to add to the suspense, a faint rectangle of gold glowed in a distant recess.

I gravitated toward the feeble light, guided by the damp wall, shoes crunching over layers of grit and ancient plaster dust. The door swung inwards on well-oiled hinges at the touch of my hand, soundless and slow. The sight that greeted me resembled a fairytale grotto more than an underground bolthole, with every inch of shelf space — and with few notable exceptions it was *all* shelf space — reflecting myriad chinks of light. Candles and oil lamps glowed from every corner. Bottles crammed shelves, apothecary jars crowded tables, various oddly-shaped receptacles were swept brutishly into the corners. And standing with his back to me in the middle of it all waited a man dressed like a refugee from the Dark Ages. His cowl and robes hung nearly to the floor. Strangely, the garment itself seemed to have been sewn together from pieces of mismatched canvas sacking instead of conventional cloth, something which put me in mind of the jury-rigged maintenance room overhead.

I made a sound — whether I drew breath or scraped the floor with my sole, I don't recall; but it was enough to alert the brooding figure to my presence. Very deliberately, and with no outward sign of a start, he turned and regarded me with eyes as cool and fathomless as inkwells.

"What do you want?" he said.

"My name is Paul Gemson," I told him, "I work as a field operative for a firm of insurance fraud investigators. A man died during a case I was on — a genuine tragedy, but one that cost me a lot of money." I held out the scrap of paper upon which Legrash's details were written. "I found this on his person."

Legrash plucked the scrap of paper from my fingers, glanced at it, passed it back. "I repeat, what is it that you want?" Before I could answer he brushed back the cowl to reveal a face gaunt with undernourishment and bone-deep weariness. The hair was cropped short to the scalp, but lay unevenly, as if Legrash cut his own hair. "You seek compensation, perhaps? As you can see," he observed, indicating the sorry state of his clothes, "I have no money of my own."

"I don't care about money," I told him, only accepting the truth now that the words were out of my mouth. "I want answers. Who was Victor Mortenson? What did he mean to you?"

"Mortenson was a fool," retorted Legrash. "Like a fool, he reacted badly when shown the error of his ways."

"But he died of a massive brain haemorrhage."

Legrash reacted not in the slightest to this.

"Hardly my concern."

"But you *were* aware of his death?"

Legrash studied me for a long time, the austerity of his expression contrasted by the crystal opulence of the shelves. Iridescent flecks of light winked at me from every angle. Finally he nodded and dropped his gaze. This seemed to dislodge something in his heart, for he began moving around the room, straightening bottles, testing their stoppered mouths. "Mortenson visited me here several weeks ago with a request for help," he admitted, checking the contents of a bell-shaped jar. "This happens from time to time. Members of the public discover my whereabouts, request my assistance. If they believe the rumours, they rarely accept the mundanity of truth."

"What rumours," I demanded, "what truth?" There was a sickly thudding in my chest, so loud and persistent that I fancied the front of my shirt jumped in time to its beat.

Legrash produced a rag from his cloak and proceeded to polish an apothecary jar that stood on a low shelf. "That I am a shaman of some kind. That I possess magical powers. The power to heal, for instance."

"And is that what —"

"Victor Mortenson had a young son who suffered from Hodgkinson's Disease. He believed I could manufacture some kind of potion to cure the child, or at least delay the inevitable."

"And did you?"

Legrash interrupted his polishing and shot me a defiant look. "I did not," he said, "that is not a part of my work. If you want to know what I do, feel free to examine one of those bottles, but do *not* touch."

I ventured beyond the threshold of the vault-like room and studied the first bottle I encountered.

Legrash said: "Tell me what is written on the label."

"Succour," I recited, allowing my eye to rove across the dusty ranks of vessels. Some of them were laced with cobwebs, others appeared shiny and new. All of them were labelled. *Vainglory*, read one, *Avarice* another. There was also *Modesty*, *Compassion*, *Prudence* and *Joy* — not to mention several hundred others. Many of the older bottles bore labels so faded that age had rendered them all but illegible. *Chivalry* was one such example. It sat alone on a high shelf in a cracked crystal decanter, and it looked almost empty. "What *is* this," I breathed, "you don't exactly manufacture cologne here, do you?"

At this Legrash threw back his head as if to roar with laughter. Instead what emerged was a bone-dry chuckle — the product, no doubt, of his perpetually covert existence. "I know nothing of perfumes," he allowed, "but I appreciate your wit, Mr Gemson. I encounter altogether too few people in my chosen vocation, and almost none with a sense of humour as rich and inveigling as yours. These," he said, taking in his entire stock with one sweep of the arm, "are the Essences. And I am their Keeper." His smile, which had broadened somewhat during the telling, receded to a vanishing point. "But that, of course, you already knew. Shall I continue?"

I told him that he should.

For a man loath to receive visitors, Legrash was all too happy to share his wisdom with a total stranger. Simply put, he claimed that when mankind moved from the countryside to the cities during the first wave of the Industrial Revolution, we left something of our true nature behind. With the help of the nation's top alchemists and physicians, a wealthy banker by the name of Walter Radbourne eventually captured and distilled that which had been lost, in the form of the Essences. *Purely for posterity's sake*, he is said to have written at the time. The project, however, continued unabated despite that initial victory. No longer content to possess all that had been lost, Radbourne further endeavoured to capture that which remained. By the mid-nineteenth century, every major town and city in the Western world had its own stock of Essences, each stock its own Keeper.

"The population right here in London has expanded so rapidly in recent years that stocks are now allocated per postal district, would you believe?"

"You're making it up," I said, actually far from convinced that he was.

"If only it were so. Unlike the seven deadly sins, the Essences are legion. Their very existence, however, is a closely guarded secret."

"But what does the Keeper *do*, exactly?"

"Do?" Legrash seemed surprised by this. He gestured at the bottles once more, a trifle perplexed. "Why, nothing. For the most part, the Keeper merely watches. Keeps guard, if you like — although most of the real guarding is done by a group of like-minded associates in higher places, members of an exclusive group originally set up by Radbourne himself in 1794. They are the ones who provide the Keeper with various sanctuaries across the city. My role is that of curator, at best."

I considered the cramped, dusty confines of the room and snorted in derision. "And this is the best these rich and powerful men can do for you? A damp burrow between floors? The life of a *mole*?"

"The Keeper must be untainted by material wealth, Mr Gemson. I can accept no more than the humblest refuge."

"That doesn't make sense." I grimaced awkwardly and licked my lips, tasting the lie. Down here in the filth and the darkness of Temple Towers, Legrash's story was starting to sound frighteningly authentic. "But you can't just guard the Essences, surely? I mean, you must do *something* with them, right?"

"On the contrary, I do as little as possible." He offered me a quirky little smile. "The facts of the matter are that the Essences do their own work. Take this bottle here."

To my astonishment, Legrash snatched up a fairly large, pear-shaped bottle filled with a pink liquid reminiscent of dental mouthwash, and spun it on his palm. "Romance," he observed, tapping the label with a horned fingernail. "Once almost empty, the contents grew and fermented until reaching their high-point around the late nineteen-fifties. I'm afraid the level has been dropping steadily ever since. Whereas the level in that receptacle over *there* has risen in direct opposition." He pointed to a cloudy specimen jar filled with what looked like stale horse piss.

"Cynicism," I read in disbelief.

"Quite."

I told him I found it all a bit difficult to accept, but was intrigued anyhow. "And you claim that all these liquids actually do is perform a barometer function of some sort, reflecting the rise and fall —"

Legrash's frown stopped me in my tracks. "Not in the slightest. The Essences do not follow, they lead. When the levels in the bottles change, so society changes in accordance. Don't ask me how or why these changes occur, but occur they do. Take the bottle of Chivalry you noticed a few moments ago. Another year and it may empty entirely. That is not a reflection, my friend. That is a fact of life."

I advanced a half-dozen paces and examined the bottle from up close.

"If what you say is true, wouldn't it be safer to turn this over to the government and be done with it? I mean, if it's as precious as you claim, security of a much higher level is required, surely?"

Legrash chuckled his dry chuckle once more. "Let me put the following scenario to you, Mr Gemson, then you may decide for yourself. Imagine that the country is knee-deep in recession. In dire financial straits, if you will. Investment is needed but given the prevailing economic climate, nobody dare take that risk. What does the Chancellor of the Exchequer do? Tamper with interest rates? Fiddle indirect taxation? Print more money? Perhaps. But what if the plan fails? I know of one possibility. The chancellor takes the bottle of Courage and mixes a few drops of it into the receptacle containing Greed. Instant, reckless abandon on the stock markets ensues." Legrash grinned a humourless grin. "It's a heady, seductive cocktail, Mr Gemson, and one guaranteed to set the City alight. No, I'm afraid the Essences shall remain here with me where they can do no harm."

This got me all riled up. "I would have to contest that, Mr Legrash. Take poor Victor Mortenson, lying dead in that alleyway. How can you call that 'doing no harm'?"

"I call it so because it is so. Mortenson caused the damage

himself, the Essences were merely his weapon of choice."

"What exactly *did* he do?" I wanted to know. I think I said it in a whisper.

"Ah, well that's the easy part. Mortenson turned up here with his tale of woe, demanding that I restore his son's health. He was quite insistent."

"And what did you say?"

"That he had paid an extortionate amount of money for a name, a location, and the illusion of hope. That I am not a doctor and am unable to work miracles." Legrash shrugged. "It didn't help. He kept telling me that he lacked determination, that he needed to be more forceful in securing the best possible treatment for his son, that his wife no longer respected him. Before I could intervene he grabbed the bottle of Ambition, downed a mouthful and departed, leaving all of his hard-earned money on the table. And there it remains."

Sure enough, several banded bundles of cash — many of them new judging by the condition of the notes — were piled at the corner of the table nearest to me.

"I thought you said you had no money of your own?"

"I do not. Perhaps you would be kind enough to take it off my hands, Mr Gemson. Or does that sound too much like a bribe?"

"Depends what you want in return," I said, calculating the value of the funds based on the denominations I could see. "How much is there, exactly?"

"I honestly wouldn't know. Would you care to count it?" Legrash retreated to the shadows at the back of the room. Heavy velvet drapes covered the far wall, and as the Keeper concluded the question he tugged on a drawstring in the corner. Darkness withdrew; light flooded the room. For a moment it was like waking from a dream, or the spell of a particularly engaging campfire tale. One minute all was magic and intrigue and limitless possibility, the next a concrete office block leapt into view. Pale dust motes danced in the clammy air. Only the money retained its former charm.

I picked up one of the bundles and fanned it with my thumb. "I think I'd like to make sure it's genuine before I go any further," I said, and joined the Legrash at the window. The building directly across the street loomed at us through the rain. It was newer than Temple Towers, and a woman with her hair done up in an ornate bun was leaning from an open window and clucking at a pigeon on a nearby ledge.

I began checking serial numbers, all of which were unique and non-sequential. My heart soon sank. There was no more than a thousand here, in notes of five, ten and twenty. Together with the other four bundles, this scarcely made a dent in the bonus I would have pulled from the blown case.

"Satisfied?"

I told him I was, even though I wasn't, and continued to stare at the woman across the street. She cooed incessantly as she gestured at the hapless pigeon, pendant earrings swinging in time to her calls. The animal tried to approach her for the crust she offered, but appeared unable to walk. You see that a lot in the cities. Urban pigeon guano contains a lot of ammonia, and standing around in it for long periods of time eats away the toes. This looked like an old bird, and all it appeared to have left were stumps.

"Tell me, Mr Legrash," I ventured, "are there any Essences you'd prefer *not* to have?"

The Keeper grunted and peered at the street. At this time of day traffic was light and the few cars in evidence glided back and forth without impediment.

"They all serve a purpose," he muttered, and with that he undid a latch, pushing the window wide. It was the kind jointed in the middle, so that the top half swung down and back while the bottom portion eased out. Cold winter wind whipped through the room, replacing the musty air with plenty of fresh, allowing outside sounds to flood in. The traffic, the woman with the earrings still making those bizarre cooing sounds, it was all much clearer.

"How about Greed?" I suggested, "Or Jealousy? Or Hate? What purpose does hate serve, Legrash?"

No sooner had I spoken than the pigeon fluttered its wings, gave the woman a nervous glance, and limped off in the opposite direction. It wasn't incapacitated after all. It was afraid.

Afraid of a good Samaritan. I experienced something of an epiphany right about then, a moment of insight so profound it left me short of breath. I realised that the universal lexicon of fear, with its near limitless power to constrict good people's hearts and deflect them from their goals, constituted our single greatest threat to well-being and prosperity. And not just for humanity, either. Take that poor, cowering pigeon. Clearly starving, it would have preferred to die than place its trust in a well-meaning stranger. We're no different, none of us. Fear of rejection, fear of failure, fear of success. A child's terror of what lurks beneath the bed. I thought about my own life and the opportunities missed because I had been too intimidated or frightened to act. It wouldn't happen again.

I stuffed the money into my pocket and made a crucial decision.

Legrash felt some of it, I think. Not the whole — I was too canny for that. But he knew what was coming. With the rainy light of afternoon on his face, light which picked out the folds and hollows of his worn skin like an inquisitive buzzard, he looked immeasurably old and fatigued.

"Get out of my sight," he muttered.

I obliged, but not before following my instincts to their logical conclusion. The bottle labelled *Fear* sat on a table between *Obedience* and *Shame*. I snatched it up, hurled it at the wall before I could think twice. It detonated with a bright flash. I think we both screamed at that point, Legrash probably more in surprise than anything else. Me, in triumph. I felt no fear at all, not a bit — only exhilaration at what I had done, and massive, overwhelming relief. The doors of perception were being yanked off their frames one hinge at a time, and the world in all of its true glory and potential came shining through. Then things began to change. The steady workaday hum of traffic in the street was usurped by the shriek of tires, as formerly considerate motorists relinquished their fear and accelerated up through the gears, engines roaring.

But that was only the beginning. As Legrash fought to recover from the momentary blindness that possessed him, the woman opposite clambered onto the narrow ledge of her building despite being more than a dozen flights above street-level. With the crust of bread clamped firmly between her teeth, she started crawling towards the pigeon without the slightest hesitation. Nobody bothered to intervene. Her colleagues were as impervious to fear as she, and were immersed in similar acts of recklessness.

As was I.

Grabbing the rest of the money, I dashed for the ladder — not to effect an escape from the madness, but to partake of it. I needed to get into the thick of it, to have my fill, to do it all, everything, right now, with no regrets.

By the time I made it outside the Isle of Dogs had erupted like a bloated pustule. Cars and taxis ploughed into shopfronts, or mowed through bus queues even as those in line argued and jostled for position. Office workers streamed from the lobbies of tall buildings, irate pedestrians snapped at one another like dogs in the street. The fires came next. The rapes and the lootings followed. The insurrection grew exponentially after that. Death meant nothing anymore; murder was commonplace.

My own role in those darkly malevolent celebrations is something that cannot be denied. Having discarded the regulatory yoke of fear, I roamed from one neighborhood to the next, sating my hunger for disorder and rebellion in all of its forms. I kicked in the display window of an off-license near Marsh Wall and gulped single malt whiskey till I puked, goaded a bunch of partying accountants into throwing their line manager from a second story office window, danced on the roofs of parked cars as their warring owners traded blows with tire irons and steering locks. Further up the same street, a voluptuous woman in an expensively-tailored suit was in the midst of performing an elaborate striptease for a delegation of Estonian businessmen when the members of a police armed response unit dragged her kicking and screaming into an alleyway, their belts already unbuckled.

I was one of the lucky ones. By some miracle of fate, my participation in the festivities took me beyond the reaches of E14 and thus beyond the boundary. The spell broke like a fever. Immediately my senses returned, and with them the horror.

On reaching home I turned on the TV and dressed my wounds the best I could. Helicopter film crews were hovering over the epicenter of the violence and commenting on how strange it was that the riots apparently ended in a ruler-straight line at the limits of the surrounding postal districts. Those who crossed the line by accident, or were dragged over against their will, suddenly seemed to awaken from a docile trance and launch headlong into the fray.

I watched the whole thing progress on CNN and Sky News, looked on in awe as men in bloodstained business suits who had inadvertently wandered into the secure zone stood around blinking and wondering how on earth they had become involved in something like this. Scant yards away citizens of all ages, colors and backgrounds beat and gouged and bludgeoned each other into submission, and in some cases even death.

I muted the broadcast and closed my eyes, the same thought going round and round in my mind. When the mess was cleared up, the government would investigate. It would track the violence back to Temple Towers, then trace it directly to its source. I imagined the chancellor and the prime minister in some dusty back room in Whitehall, dressed in lab coats and goggles as they mixed samples of the Essences into cocktails of triumph and prosperity, innovation and leadership. Anything their hearts desired.

The carnage already witnessed will pale in comparison the day those experiments are complete. And such a day is coming sooner than we think.

Just look at the way politics is going now.

BLOODBATH AT LANDSDALE TOWERS
by Michael Boatman

Danny Wahlberg, twenty-one, white, and dumb as a box of chicken turds, cleared his throat, blinked three times and said: "You want me to do *what?*"

Lennox Ravanaugh, thirty-nine, black, and mean as a Republican with a rattlesnake up his dickhole, held up one of a dozen little plastic packets that sat on the table in front of him.

"I said I want you to fuck your sister in the ass."

White Bitch — who had once answered to the name Carrie-Ellen Wahlberg but now answered simply to White Bitch — shook her blond head and pulled a knife.

"You stay the fuck away from me, Danny."

Ravanaugh looked back and forth between the twins. They were good for a few more weeks at least. He chuckled and sniffed the little packet.

"Bubble bubble toil and trouble," he said.

The packet held five chunks of rock cocaine. When smoked, they would produce the kind of chemical satisfaction that squirmed its way down into your DNA, checked out the accommodations and said "Make Room For Daddy."

"Weeeelll?" Ravanaugh sang.

Danny glanced over at his sister, who had certainly seen better days.

"Don't even think about it, Danny," White Bitch said. "I'll cut your fucking nuts off."

Danny shook his head and turned back to Ravanaugh.

"I don't think she's gonna go for it."

Ravanaugh smirked. "Well that's a shame," he said. "Ain't it, fellas?"

Ravanaugh's Crew, a ragtag motley made up of some of the

stupidest humans on Earth, made cattle sounds.

Goat, Ravanaugh's best runner, cackled and spat out two of his teeth. The teeth hit the cheap linoleum and bounced under the sofa like a pair of rotten dice. Rook, Lil' Knot and Pabo, Ravanaugh's lieutenants, laughed and threw used condoms at each other.

"Yo, Goat," Ravanaugh said.

He flicked the packet over his shoulder.

Goat was nineteen years old and looked sixty, but he scampered across the room with the dexterity that only lifelong junkies can muster and caught the packet before it hit the floor.

"Hell yeah, boss," he panted. "Hell yeah."

Goat produced a pipe and lit up. A sound like a fresh sucking chest wound filled apartment 1654. Then Goat leaned back and closed his eyes.

Danny Wahlberg drooled on his sneakers.

"Sis," he whined.

"No, Danny," White Bitch said. "The hand-job was bad enough."

But White Bitch was weakening. She backed up onto the mattress that served as Goat's palette. The mattress smelled like the septic field of a Mexican abortion clinic at high tide. White Bitch's blade dipped. Her attention fluttered between Danny and the Goat.

Ravanaugh heaved a contented sigh.

"Ah, nothing stokes my juices quite like snappin' the moral backbone of upper middle-class privilege."

Ravanaugh lived for grinding down the ones from Chicago's Northern suburbs, the ones whose parents sucked ass for Haliburton or Exxon or any of the mega-corps that were cornholing the planetary working class.

By 2010 raging unemployment, abetted by four successive Bush administrations, had forged a Darwinian nightmare for the residents of the Landsdale Towers Residential Estates.

The gauntlet of drug dealers, crack whores and child molesters that stalked the seven-mile stretch of State Street that contained the L.T.R.E, made life in the projects as pleasant as crawling through the anal tract of a rabid she-moose at the height of mating season.

The college basketball scouts made it worse.

But any guilt Ravanaugh might have felt — since he ran the criminal operations that centered around the Towers — paled beside his outrage at the depredations of Corporate America.

"See, fellas?" Ravanaugh said. "A middle-class white kid'll shank his grandmama if you fuck with his sense of entitlement. Observe."

Ravanaugh swept the packets off the tabletop and into the open briefcase on his lap. He snapped the briefcase shut. Danny jumped as if Ravanaugh had fired a shotgun.

"Gimme that briefcase, you cunt," White Bitch snarled. "Or I'll stick this knife up your fat ass."

Lil' Knot and Pabo snickered. Over in the corner, the Goat nodded and fell off of his chair.

"Last chance, Dan," Ravanaugh said. "How 'bout it?"

Danny turned and lurched, zombie-like, toward White Bitch. White Bitch whirled and slashed a long red gash from his inner elbow to his palm. Danny howled.

"Owww!"

He smacked White Bitch across the jaw, knocking the knife across the room. White Bitch swung a booted foot up and caught Danny square in the balls. Danny let out a *whooof*, clutched himself and dropped face-first onto the
mattress.

"Bravo," Ravanaugh said. Then he picked up a packet and held it out to White Bitch. She reached for it.

"Ah ah ahhh," Ravanaugh whispered.

White Bitch hesitated. Ravanaugh lifted the packet and sniffed it.

"Mmmmmhhh *goooood*," he said.

White Bitch unzipped her jeans and went over to the mattress. Ravanaugh laughed, his barrel chest filling the room with bad humor.

"We should have brought hay," he said.

"White folks are so fucking *depraved*."

***

Ravanaugh was just about to make White Bitch blow the whole Crew when someone knocked on the door.

Danny was lying on the mattress with his underpants
around his ankles. White Bitch was trying to crawl out from under Mosquito. Mosquito, who was diabetic, had passed out on top of White Bitch while pounding her into a thin paste on the cheap industrial-strength carpet. Mosquito weighed nearly four-hundred pounds: White Bitch lay spread-eagled beneath a fifth of a ton of insulin-resistant mocha man-mountain.

Ravanaugh said, "See who it is."

Rook, Ravanaugh's second-in-command, strode over to
the door, a Glock nine mm gripped in his fist.

"Who the fuck is it?" Rook shouted.

"A better question might be: Who the heck are you?"

Ravanaugh and Crew spun around.

A black man wearing a long, camel-brown duster and a white ten-gallon hat was standing in the doorway to the bedroom.

"Who the fuck are you?" Ravanaugh said. "How the fuck did you get in here?"

Duster shook his head. "Mister, you sure got a dirty mouth."

Ravanaugh stared at the stranger.

He appeared middle-aged and stood about six-two, maybe six-three. His chest and shoulders were broad, his middle free of anything resembling fat. Duster looked like the sort of man who got his exercise ripping boulders out of the earth with his bare hands.

The Crew drew down. Duster didn't seem to notice.

"What's with that fucked up outfit?" Ravanaugh said.

Duster made a tsking sound.

"Anybody ever tell you fellas it ain't polite to say the F-word s'much?" he said. "'Specially in the presence of a lady?"

"What lady — ?" Ravanaugh said.

Duster nodded toward the front door.

The woman standing in the doorway might not have been Eartha Kitt's younger, hotter sister but she surely could have passed for her.

"Hello, boys."

She was wearing a red leather catsuit.

Red stiletto heels put the woman at about six feet two inches tall. She was the color of milk chocolate, her short black hair combed backward and slicked down. She had the blackest eyes Ravanaugh had ever seen.

Ravanaugh's eyes darted back and forth between the invaders like a man watching someone play tennis with his balls. "Who are you people?" he said.

Duster stepped forward and took his hat off.

"My name is Nathaniel Corners. That over there's my associate, Miss Negrita Marcos."

"Negrita?" Pabo said. "Que tu quiere, mama?"

Negrita bowed smoothly from the hips and answered him in

Spanish. Her voice was heavy, dusky, like her skin.

"She said they come a long way to meet *you*, boss," Pabo said.

Negrita smiled. Her teeth were very, *very* white.

"You are Lenny Ravanaugh," Corners said. "But on the street they call you Highball."

"*Lenny*," Lil' Knot snorted.

Corners laughed. Ravanaugh's gut tightened and his mouth went dry.

That's not a man standing there, he thought. *Nothing like a man and you know it, don't you?*

"Hey, Ravanaugh. What's happenin'?"

Ravanaugh turned to see Danny rising to his feet. The male twin looked like he'd been drinking cat piss in a fall-out shelter for the last three months.

"Who the fuck is this clown?" he said.

Corners stopped chuckling. His smile winked out of existence: There was no gradual relaxing of facial muscles. It was simply there one moment and gone the next.

"I don't cotton to that kind of talk," Corners said.

Danny shrugged and pulled up his shorts.

"Let me gank this asshole, Naugh," Rook said.

He lifted his Glock and aimed it at Corners. Lil' Knot and Pabo followed suit.

"Chill," Ravanaugh said. "Let's hear the man out."

"Yo, this is bullshit," Danny said. I don't have to listen to this asshole."

Corners turned toward Danny and said: "You call me outta my name one more time, sonny-jim, and you're gonna call down the thunder."

Danny lifted his middle finger.

"Fuck. You. *Asshole*."

"Wait ..." Ravanaugh said.

Corners' right arm moved and something flicked past his Ravanaugh's ear. Then Danny's hands flew up and fluttered against his face like startled doves.

"Get it off get it off get it off me!" he screamed.

Blood splashed down the fronts of Danny's arms, streaked

his white skin with slashes of red as gouts of flesh flew from between his clenched fists. He screamed and fell to the floor.

"What's happening?" White Bitch squeaked. "Danny?"

Danny arched and bucked on the floor, his head and heels drumming on bare cement where the linoleum had worn through. Then he lay still. A single robin's egg-blue eye glared at Ravanaugh through a mask of blood. The other half of Danny's face was a gaping red crater.

"Son of a bitch," Rook whispered.

Then something climbed out of Danny's eye socket.

It was the size and shape of a hockey puck. A dozen black spider's legs extended out of the thing. It rose up on those perfect black legs, skittered up Danny's forehead and settled on the crown of his skull.

Two legs scooped out a chunk of Danny's eye socket and smeared it into a pink slit along the top of the hockey puck. Ravanaugh saw a tiny black tongue slide out of the slit and lap up the red glob.

"Bullshit," Ravanaugh said.

Pabo and Lil' Knot scrambled past the woman in red and fled down the hallway. Rook lifted his Glock.

Negrita *moved.* Ravanaugh was still staring at the empty doorway before he realized she was gone. He spun: Negrita was standing *behind* Rook. She grabbed his right arm and wrenched it up behind his back. Then she grabbed him by the scruff of the neck, bent him forward and yanked his arm over his head, lifting him up onto his toes.

"Let me go, you crazy bitch!" Rook said.

"Oooh," Negrita purred. "Talk dirty to me, pusher man."

Then she broke his arm —

Crack

— and Rook screamed and dropped his gun.

Negrita drew back her fist and punched Rook in the back of the head. The front of his face *pooched* outward from the force of the blow. Hydrostatic pressure did the rest: Rook's forehead exploded and spattered the floor with thirty-five years' worth of bad news.

"Danny?" White Bitch screamed. "I can't breathe!"

Over in the corner, Mosquito had slipped into a diabetic coma. White Bitch was stuck.

Corners seemed intent on enjoying Negrita's display. His laughter sliced the air like ravens' wings.

"Now that's what I call black comedy," he said. "Wouldn't you agree, Ravanaugh?"

Lil' Knot and Pabo were gone, but Ravanaugh knew they would have to pass two-dozen killers on their way down to the street. He congratulated himself on having had the foresight to murder all the local gangleaders; it had made hiring their homeboys as his personal guard that much simpler. Ravanaugh could almost hear his 'kill squad' thundering toward them now.

Money well spent, he thought. *Any second now.*

Even with Death staring him in the face, however, Ravanaugh remained a businessman. Life and Death were his business and there was always another angle to exploit.

"What's next?" he said.

Corners turned, one eyebrow raised. "How's that?"

Ravanaugh shrugged. "Since I'm still suckin' wind I figure y'all must want something I have. Let's conversate."

Negrita draped her arm across his shoulders.

"We want information," she said.

Ravanaugh's nose crinkled: Negrita smelled of perfume, something fruity, like the stuff his more upscale call girls used before meeting a "date," but beneath the perfume lurked another smell, something that made Ravanaugh think of fresh roadkill on a hot summer day.

"What kind of — of information?" he said.

Corners strode over to where Goat lay unconscious on the floor. He bent down, his brow furrowed, and shook his head. Then he whistled.

The hockey puck that killed Danny Wahlberg rolled across the floor, leaving a trail of blood in its wake. The Death Puck stopped at Goat's high-top sneakers. Then it climbed up Corners' leg and disappeared into his pocket.

Corners pulled a Smith & Wesson Model 19 Combat Magnum out of a holster on his left hip, thumbed back the hammer, and said, "This one's done."

Ravanaugh's roar of outrage was drowned out by the blast as Corners blew Goat's head apart.

"Names," Corners said.

"You're crazy, motherfucker!"

"Ah ah ah," Negrita said. "Profanity is the last refuge of the weak-minded."

"Fuck you, bitch!"

Corners stepped over Goat's body.

"I warned you," he said.

Then he ripped Ravanaugh's ear off.

Ravanaugh screamed as blood jumped out of his head and spattered the right shoulder of his new Armani running suit. He fell to his knees, stomach heaving as bile burned a fireline up the back of his throat.

Help me, he thought. *Where are they?*

Negrita picked up his ear and pocketed it. Then she slid a long-bladed dagger from a sheathe on her ankle and started *doing things* to the three corpses. Ravanaugh gagged.

Corners leaned down and spoke softly.

"Let me make it plain for you, sonny-jim," he said.

He grabbed Ravanaugh's right wrist, raised his hand to eye-level and grabbed his index finger.

"You will provide the names and phone numbers of every dealer, every runner, every contact you currently employ."

Ravanaugh's eyes widened. "You must be outta your goddamned — "

POP

Ravanaugh snarled, bit back his scream. Corners released the finger he'd broken and grabbed its neighbor.

"You will provide this information post haste, or I'll call Nat Jr. out to play, and believe me, Nat Jr.'s gonna do more than pop a few knuckles, right son?"

The Death puck climbed up onto Corners' shoulder and shrieked. To Ravanaugh, Nat Jr. sounded like a monkey with a throat full of razor blades.

Something warm and wet landed on Ravanaugh's forehead and settled over his left eye. Half blind, Ravanaugh broke.

"Please," he said. "Get it off me."

"Nat Jr. likes you," Corners said. "Findin' the right playmate for your pups is so important these days."

Nat Jr. stroked Ravanaugh's left eyelid with one of his legs. Ravanaugh began to cry.

"In — in my briefcase," he said. "My — my phone. It's got all the names and numbers on it."

Negrita retrieved the briefcase and opened it. Inside lay twelve-thousand dollars worth of powder and rock cocaine, along with two handguns and three wireless phones.

"Easy peezy," Negrita said.

She put the items she'd harvested from the two dead men, along with Ravanaugh's ear, in the briefcase. Danny's blue eyeball winked at Ravanaugh before Negrita shut the lid.

"Witch's brew," she hummed.

Ravanaugh looked up at Corners. "P — please don't kill me."

"Alright," Corners said.

He stepped back. Then Negrita yanked Ravanaugh's head back and sliced his jugular. Ravanaugh clutched at his throat, trying to staunch the blood gushing between his fingers.

"Somebody — help —," he sputtered.

Then he dropped.

The strangers stood in the center of the room with their eyes closed. Outside, a passing pigeon blew apart in a shower of blood and feathers.

Corners moved first.

"Okay then," he said.

Negrita said, "Had enough?"

Nat Jr. shrieked, curled itself into a ball and slipped back into Corners' pocket.

"Not quite done," Corners said. "But we should move on."

Corners strode out into the hallway and headed toward the elevator. Negrita hefted the briefcase, but a flicker of motion caught her eye. She whirled, knife in hand.

A smile lit up Negrita's supermodel face.

"Oh ho," she grinned. "What have we here?"

The woman in red glided across the room to where White Bitch peered out from beneath her fleshy prison.

Negrita chuckled. "You look like you're wearing a babushka

made out of chocolate-covered chitlin's."

She kicked Mosquito in the ribs. Her boot disappeared up to the ankle in a gelatinous fold near his armpit.

"What — the — hell?" Mosquito grunted.

Negrita leaned down and sniffed.

"Diabetic," she said. "Asshole."

Then she jammed her knife into Mosquito's right ear. Mosquito shuddered and vomited all over White Bitch. Negrita grimaced and rolled him off of the girl.

"Hello, treasure," she said. "What's your name?"

"White —" White Bitch shook her head and cleared her throat — "I mean — Carrie-Ellen Wahlberg, ma'am."

Negrita stooped and helped Carrie-Ellen stand up.

"Let's get you out of here, honey," she said.

"My — my brother," Carrie-Ellen said.

"Dead, I'm afraid," Negrita said. "Best not to look."

Carrie-Ellen accepted the bad news as gracefully as a woman wearing a body fluid cocktail dress can.

"Fuck this," she said.

"Language, dear," Negrita said.

Corners was waiting at the elevator.

"Look what I found, partner," Negrita sang.

Corners smiled. The elevator doors slid open.

"Whoa," Corners said.

The shaft was empty. No elevator waited beyond the doors. Arnold Schwarzenegger's *Terminator* glared at Corners, emblazoned in silver and red on the back wall of the shaft. A lightless abyss stretched away beneath his feet.

"Pity the children," Corners said.

A volley of curses erupted from apartment 1646.

"Better hurry," Negrita said.

"What are we gonna do?" Carrie-Ellen said.

Corners extended his right hand.

"Trust me, baby doll?"

Carrie-Ellen nodded. She placed her small pink hand in Corners' big brown one. Then Corners whipped her around and threw her into the elevator shaft. Carrie-Ellen bounced off the back wall and fell screaming into the darkness.

"Now I'm done," Corners said.

From around the corner, the sounds of a posse filled the hallway. Corners extended his left hand.

"Shall we, milady?"

Negrita gripped the briefcase in her left hand and gave Corners her right. Together, they stepped into the elevator shaft and went up, Corners' duster flapping behind him like wings in the darkness.

They held hands as they rose.

BIOGRAPHICAL INFORMATION

Gerard Brennan

Born in the summer of '79, Gerard Brennan lives in a small seaside town in the North of Ireland with his beautiful wife Michelle and his incredible daughter Mya. When he is not studying to become a soulless accountant he writes dark fiction and bad poetry. He also writes kung fu movie reviews for www.steelsamurai.co.uk.

To keep tabs on his writing success (or lack thereof) visit http://gerardbrennan.livejournal.com.

Garry Kilworth

Garry Kilworth has published over 120 short stories and 70 novels, much of them in Fantasy and Science Fiction genres. He travels a great deal, mostly in the Far East, with a backpack on his back and his wife Annette by his side. While on these journeys he likes to dig dark myths and legends out of the cultures with which he comes into contact. His most recent books are *Brothers of the Blade*, an historical war novel set in India, and *Attica* a dark quest set in an attic the size of a continent.

Michael Hemmingson

Michael Hemmingson's latest books are *Harmony* (Blue Moon), *The Yacht People* (Neon/Orion Publishing) and *Expelled from Eden: A William T. Vollmann Reader* (Thunder's Mouth Press). He lives in San Diego, California, where he battles racoon vampires and time traveling invaders from the past.

Ronald Damien Malfi

Ronald Damien Malfi is a novelist and screenwriter whose short fiction has appeared in countless print and online magazines, collections, and anthologies. His novel, *The Fall of Never*, was released in 2004 to critical acclaim. Gothic Revue proclaimed, "The Fall of Never is a masterpiece all on its own, a continuous piecing together of mind puzzles," while Midwest Book Review hailed it as "one of the most enthralling and nail-biting books I've read in years!" His two upcoming novels include the highly anticipated *Via Dolorosa* and *The Nature of Monsters*. He lives in Annapolis, Maryland with his wife, Debra, who is almost a doctor.

Gord Rollo

Gord Rollo has many short story sales in both professional and semi-professional markets. His first novel, *Crimson*, originally released by Prime Books, was reprinted by specialty press, The Midnight Library, in January of 2006. His new novel, *Jigsaw*, will be released in limited edition hardcover by Delirium Books in June of 2006, and then released in paperback later in the year. Besides novels, Gord edited the acclaimed evolutionary horror anthology, *Unnatural Selection: A Collection of Darwinian Nightmares*. He also co-edited *Dreaming of Angels*, a horror/fantasy anthology to raise money and awareness for Downs Syndrome. He's currently hard at work on his latest novel, *Strange Magic*.

Davin Ireland

Davin Ireland currently resides in the Netherlands. His fiction credits include stories published in a range of print magazines and anthologies, including *Underworlds*, *Revelation*, *Hoodz*, *The Horror Express*, *Neo-Opsis*, *Black Petals*, *Here & Now*, *Zahir*, *Albedo One*, *JPPN2*, *Dark Animus*, *The Blackest Death Volume II*, and *Futures Mysterious Anthology Magazine*.

Michael Boatman

Michael Boatman is also proud of his day job. As an actor, he co-starred in the television series *Spin City* and the HBO series *Arliss*. He has appeared in many television programs like *Law and Order S.V.U.*, and feature films, including *Kalamazoo, Woman Thou Art Loosed, The Glass Shield, The Peacemaker,* and *Hamburger Hill*. His short fiction appears in *Horror Garage, Red Scream,* and in the upcoming anthologies, *Dark Dreams II: Voices From the Other Side; Daikaiju II! Return of the Giant Monster Tales!;* and *Sages and Swords*. He is currently at work on his third novel, and several film projects.

Printed in the United Kingdom
by Lightning Source UK Ltd.
111166UKS00001B/22